Isadora Stone

and

The Battle for Inner Earth

Laura Anne Whitworth

Cover Artwork by Gemma Louise Banks

Copyright© 2019 by Laura Anne Whitworth

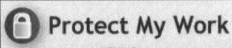

Acknowledgements

My rock, my world, my husband. Always constant, always supportive. Always my calm when all around me is crumbling. My love for you is infinite.

My daughters. You are my light. Thank you for giving Mummy a purpose. With lots of laughs, fun, snuggles and kisses along the way.

My ever supportive parents. Thanks for putting up with all my 'fads' over the years. Hopefully the writing of these books has proven that 'I can do it.'

I love you all. Forever and always.

Prelude

How would you feel, if everything that you had been told was fiction, was actually fact?
That the film Independence Day which you watched last night with your new love interest, in some reality,
actually happened?
That Bigfoot and the Henderson's was real, to some family, in some time.
That Star Trek and Stargate Atlantis is actually happening right now.
That Stargates are in fact 'a thing'.
That the fiction came from fact.
That 'the fact' is happening all around you right now.
A 'hidden' and 'cloaked' world.
Where star ships fly through our skies and aliens fight each other.
It's actually happening.
And the human race is controlled.
But you don't 'see' it.
You are too busy getting ready for work.
Too busy putting in overtime so you can afford to buy the kids what they want for Christmas.
Too busy, doing homework or studying for exams.
Exams that will help you get a good job, and earn lots of money.
Money that pays for bills.
You're too busy doing what you have always done.
Day in day out.
Getting up, going to school, going to work, coming home, having tea, going to bed.

Doing it all again.

And again.

Over and over.

Until there is a distraction which makes you feel better about your life.

It's Christmas, or Thanks giving, or a trip to the Caribbean or a holiday to Disney World with the kids.

And you breathe the fresh air again.

This is what you do it all for, right?

You feel the sun on your skin. You swim in the sea and start to notice nature again.

You feel joy enter your soul again.

Where had it been before?

Has the world always been this beautiful you muse over a glass of wine.

Staring at your partner that you have just started to see as a human again.

Then the magic ends.

It has to end as you have to go back to work.

You have to go back to work to earn more money to pay more bills.

You have to go back to school to learn more stuff.

To take more exams, to get a good job.

To earn more money, to pay more bills.

This is your life.

What if I told you it could end?

This cycle of misery could end right now?

All we have to do, is open our eyes and 'see'.

Really 'see'

There is a better way.

Let's start now.

The Beginning

Dr Evelyn Osbourne took a quick slurp of coffee and adjusted her bra strap.

How many patients was that today now?

She looked at the clock. 11.00am already and two patients down. One more she sighed then I can go get lunch. I am starving, she thought.

She checked her appointment book. 11.00am, *Brittney Jeffers*. Hmmmm Evelyn thought, a newbie today. Wonder what this one is going to bring with them! Stopping smoking? Hate their Daddy? Bullied as a kid and can't get over it?

Evelyn sighed, she was getting far too jaded with this job she thought. She had come into this field to 'make a difference'. Doesn't everyone? Yet years and years of listening to the same things had made her hard, and cynical. She had tried to help. She had really, really wanted to help. But how many people had she 'actually' helped? I can't *wait* till 5.00pm when I can open that bottle of wine that is currently chilling in my fridge, Evelyn thought. Little shivers of excitement ran up her back.

The intercom on her desk buzzed.

'Yes Mary,' Evelyn sighed accepting the inevitable.

'Your 11.00am is here Dr Osbourne,' Mary droned.

'Send her in, Mary.' Evelyn opened Brittney's file. It was blank. She pulled her skirt down as it had ridden up, adjusted her blouse and popped the end in on her pen. Put on that smile Evelyn, she reminded herself.

The door opened and in walked a small, dowdy woman. She looked to be about 40 years old; her aura and demeanor gave out the impression that she had the weight of the world on her shoulders. She was pale, skinny and wore an outsized cream overcoat which covered up everything she was wearing underneath. Out of this coat popped two skinny legs.

'Hi Brittney, please take a seat.' Evelyn gestured to the hard chesterfield chair which was directly in front of her.

'My name is Dr Evelyn Osbourne as I'm sure you are already aware,' Evelyn smiled encouragingly. 'Why don't you go ahead and in your own words tell me why you are here today and what I can help you with.' I might have the cheese salad for lunch Evelyn thought, as her stomach reminded her again that it was almost lunchtime.

The skinny, pale woman looked down at her hands and fidgeted. She was picking the skin at the side of one of her nails with increased vigour.

Any time today Evelyn thought, and her thoughts returned again to cheese salad.

'Ah, I guess I just need to talk through with a professional, what happened that day.' Brittney said in a soft, sad, timid voice.

'Why don't you go ahead and explain what you mean by *that* day Brittney,'said Evelyn. Just get on with it already she thought. The quicker we get into it, the quicker I can get my lunch. Screw the cheese salad I may pick up some fried chicken Evelyn thought, immediately feeling guilty as she thought of her thighs.

'The day that Zackary Marshall went missing,' the sad, thin woman said quietly.

'Who is Zackary Marshall, Brittney?' Evelyn leaned forward in her seat.

'He was a boy in my class.' Brittney started to sob, quietly.

'Go ahead, it's OK, this is a safe space.' Evelyn was starting to pay more attention to the pale, thin woman.

After what seemed like an age, Brittney, took a deep breath and started talking.

'It happened on a school field trip.' She said in a sad, timid voice. 'I remember like it was yesterday. It was hot, so hot. One of those days where you could feel the sweat trickling down your back. We were on a school trip to the Grand Canyon,' she laughed. But it was a sad laugh. 'Zackary Marshall had been bullying everyone on the bus on the way there. Nobody dare stand up to him. He, he had a way of finding out what your weaknesses were and exploiting them. We heard that his Mummy and Daddy were cruel to him and I guess he just did the same thing to everyone else that he came across too. There was one boy, Jacob Winters who he always picked on the most.' She started to cry again remembering the events. 'He did some really horrible things to poor Jacob. We all tried to stick up for him where we could, but at the end of the day, you didn't stand up to Zackary Marshall, not unless you wanted him to start noticing you instead. *Nobody* wanted Zackary Marshall to notice them,' Brittney sniveled.

'OK, go on.' Evelyn urged impatiently but you would never have known it in the simpering tone of her voice. She had perfected that voice.

'When we got to the Grand Canyon we all filed off the bus and waited for a guide to take us round. The guide started taking us round. It was such a hot day and people were getting bored. They weren't really listening to what the tour guy was saying. Zackary kept tripping Jacob up.' Brittney's eyes filled with tears again and it looked like she was going to resume crying.

Jeez thought Evelyn, will we ever get to the end of this story?

'He did it a couple of times, but on the third or fourth time, Jacob really fell hard and he smashed his nose on the ground. His nose was really bleeding, there was blood everywhere.' Brittney's sobs increased.

Some kid got a nose bleed? This is what this is all about Evelyn thought and she sat back in her chair and tapped her nails.

'This really made Jacob angry, mostly Jacob just took it, whatever Zackary did to him. He just stood there and took it. But for some reason today he didn't. He was real mad.' Brittney took in a large breath and leant forward to take a sip of water out of the glass that was in front of her on the table. She wiped at a trail of snot that was threatening to drop out of her nose across the back of her cream cuff.

'Jacob stood up and he kind of screamed, it was almost like a wail. Anyway he started running towards Zackary, and we just knew, we knew what he was going to do.'

'What did he do Brittney?' Evelyn asked. Finally this was getting interesting.

Brittney took in a deep breath and put her hand on her chest, as if she thought her chest was going to burst open.

'It's OK, Brittney, just say it nice and slow,' reassured Evelyn. She leant forward in her chair once more.

Brittney swallowed and her eyes glazed over as she recalled the events of her past.

'Jacob charged towards Zackary with this crazy look in his eye and you could see that Zachary realised at the same time what Jacob was going to do. Jacob ran at him hollering and screaming and ...pushed him.'

'Jacob pushed Zachary?' Evelyn questioned.

'Yes, Jacob pushed Zachary, but Zachary was too close to the edge. And he fell backwards.' Brittney started sobbing again.

'Jacob pushed Zachary off the edge of the Grand Canyon?' Evelyn clarified. Jeez no wonder this woman was upset she thought. That was nasty.

'Yes and No,' Brittney sobbed.

Yes and No? Evelyn thought, what the hell does that mean?

'Jacob pushed Zachary, and he fell backwards, towards the edge, but we all saw what happened.' Brittney said in an angry voice. 'They tried to tell us we didn't and the trauma made us see something that didn't happen in order to cover up the horror of what really happened or some other bull crap like that. But we all knew what we saw!' Brittney cried.

'What did you see?' Evelyn asked looking at Brittney with interest. Her fried chicken was long forgotten.

'Zachary disappeared!' Brittney screamed.

'He disappeared?' Whispered Evelyn. 'I don't understand?'

'Jacob pushed Zachary towards the edge of the Canyon, but he didn't fall off, he disappeared, into thin air. He was falling backwards and this, like shimmering bubble appeared in the air. It was all sparkling and rainbow colours. Zachary fell back into it and he just....disappeared!' Brittney hiccupped and fresh tears ran down her face.

Fantastic! Thought Evelyn as she sighed and sat back in her seat. What a build-up. I thought that was going to be a good one. Zachary disappeared into thin air. Of course he did.

Evelyn's thoughts returned to fried chicken.

Inner Earth

Isadora could not sleep. She had been in a funny mood all day. Like something bad was going to happen, but nothing had. There was an electricity in the air. You could almost taste it. But nothing of any consequence had happened at all.

She had spent the day shopping with her Momma. Mrs Stone had spent 3 hours excitedly searching through sales rails in Walmart for 'bargains' in Isadora's size. Isadora had tried more clothes on today than she would have needed in a year. However she only left with a new pair of slacks and a handful of T Shirts. Clothes weren't Isadora's thing at all. Obviously she knew that she needed to wear them! But she'd be happy in her favourite worn old T Shirt that her Daddy had bought for her, some slacks and her sneakers every day.

As she lay in bed, willing sleep to come to her, her thoughts turned to her Daddy. She missed him so much. It was an ache in her chest that never went away. The years passed, but her love for him stayed strong and grew. What had happened to him? She had asked this question a million times. Over and over. But the question never got answered and she had to accept that she would probably never find out. All she did know is he had gone out one day to buy groceries for them all, and he had never come back.

She knew that he would not have just left them. He would never have done that. Not her Daddy. He loved her and her Momma dearly. She knew that in her heart. She felt it. They had been so close. Her chest felt tight and her eyes welled up with the familiar hot ache of tears. The pain in her chest was all consuming.

Her thoughts were interrupted by a blinding flash of light and a huge loud BANG!
She flinched and covered her face, what on Earth?
When she opened her eyes, she stared in disbelief.

She was sat on a chair at a long stone table, in what looked to be a HUGE vast cavern.

Around the table were a variety of humans in various different outfits. There were also a couple of faces that Isadora would not describe as human. She had never seen anything like them before. She closed her mouth as she realised that her mouth was open in shock. There was a being seated at the opposite end of the table she was sat at, directly opposite her, which had purple skin! He also had a very unusual face. Sitting next to this being was a tall guy with bright green skin! He also looked to have huge gills on the side of his neck and his skin was very amphibian looking. Interesting. Uncomfortably she realised she was sitting at the head of the table. All eyes were on her.

Suddenly she became aware of the person to her left, it was Orion. She felt a happy bubble of excitement swell in her chest as she quickly wiped the tears from her cheeks. It had only been 4 weeks since they had returned from Delavia, but to Isadora it had seemed like a very long time indeed. The summer was passing very slowly with no school and no Chinga to talk to. Orion was looking particularly fantastic today in a Black and White Cowboy outfit, with, oh my goodness were those chaps? Isadora blushed and remembered her current attire.

She was sat at the head of the table in a pink nighty and bed socks and nothing else.

She wanted to die.

Peets

Peets had watched in horror and disbelief as Nathan had beaten David to the floor. The little boy did not get back up again.

What is he doing? Screamed Peets inside. I have to help him. What can I do?

The piercing sound of the guard's whistle broke through Peets' panicked thoughts. The portly guard who was sat in the watch tower today had seen the altercation from above. He was currently trying to maneuver his cumbersome frame as quickly as he could down the tower to break up the fight.

As the guard negotiated the steps of the tower, Peets saw a long dark haired girl grab hold of Nathan and spin him towards her. Peets was too far away to hear what words had been spoken between the two, but whatever the girl had said to Nathan had embarrassed him. Nathan nodded to his two friends and the trio stormed off to the other side of the exercise pen.

Peets watched as the girl lent down to speak to David and slowly checked his pulse. The girl pushed David's hair out of his eyes and pulled him towards her in an embrace, just as the guard hit the ground and fired the whistle again.

The girl jumped back quickly from David's small frame and laid him gently back on the ground. She disappeared into the crowd of humans watching what was unfolding.

The guard bent down and looked at the little boy who had thankfully began to rub his face.

He's coming round thought Peets. Thank the creator for that. I thought we had lost him.

The portly guard pulled his radio out of his waistband and began to summon extra help. He looked panicked as he tried to contain the situation.

Peets watched as two guards ran out of the door to the exercise pen and began lifting David to his feet.

The little boy looked so small, even smaller than the last time Peets had seen him. Where are they taking him? He wondered.

As Peets watched the two guards leading David across the exercise yard and back into the metal compound, his little heart started beating faster. What did he do now? If he couldn't speak with David, this would set their plan back considerably. Should he try and talk to someone else and see if they would help him?

A voice inside Peets told him No.

No he must wait for David.

The creator brought him to David.

And now David depended on him.

They depended on each other.

He would wait as long as it took for his new friend. He would come here every day and just wait.

Wait until David was well again.

It was only a little delay in their plans.

What would Koro say?

Valdazar

Valdazar sat in his special throne made of Serantium, stroking his long black moustache and beard. He did this a lot. It helped calm him down. But he also did it as he thought it made him look very important. He didn't understand it. He didn't understand it at all. How did she do it? Who *was* she? Well he knew who she was. He had sent his scouts out to find out what had happened on Delavia and who this blonde girl was. At first no-one would spill anything. No-one would talk. This made him hopping mad. But it's surprising what a bit of torture will do. Valdazar smiled. He had hired a Sasquatch deserter whom his Valdons had found drinking in a bar on Unatron. There were a few of them kicking around the Cosmos. It seems not all Sasquatch are hooked on honey and the beauty of Delavia sneered Valdazar. Some liked beer too. All he'd had to do was get this Sasquatch drunk enough to agree to go back to Delavia and fetch one of the Sasquatch there back through the portal.

That Sasquatch was now currently in Valdazars dungeon resting off a recent beating. It had taken them ages to track the two Sasquatch down as the portal on Delavia was now defective. It wasn't working properly. They were lucky that their Sasquatch deserter had managed to make it into Delavia at all. They weren't so lucky on the way out. Fortunately as Valdazar was so brilliant, he'd had the Valdons fit the Sasquatch deserter with a tracker, just in case he had tried to run. And it was due to this tracker that they had managed to locate them on an entirely different planet than the one that they were supposed to meet up on.

The hapless Delavian Sasquatch that was currently in Valdazar's dungeon had eventually spilled his guts. *Apparently* this blonde girl that he'd seen talking to the fat Ancients on his Smart Glass pad wasn't the one in charge. *Apparently* there had been another tall blonde woman with this skinny blonde girl who had definitely been in charge. Probably the girl's Mother Valdazar concluded. So the skinny blonde girl was still not off the hook. One thing is for sure thought Valdazar. I will not have a *woman* make me look stupid, he seethed. He had already had to speak with Anubis and tell him that he could no longer supply him with any additional honey from Delavia. This had made him very mad. Very mad indeed. As now Anubis thought he was stupid. And worst, that he was *weak*. And if Valdazar didn't get that honey pipeline back for him quickly, he might also even have to give Anubis back his ship. He could not do that. WOULD not do that. He loved that ship.

Valdazar was not weak!

White hot fury coursed through his veins.

He let out an angry laugh as he thought of the kicker.

Do you know what the best part is? Festered Valdazar.

The Sasquatch currently whimpering in his dungeon had said that these blond women had come from Earth.

Earth.

Earth

This planet keeps coming back to haunt me, Valdazar worried.

I cannot let them get away with this. I am Valdazar. I have to *be* Valdazar.

'Human!' Screamed Valdazar as he plotted his next move.

'Yes Sire,' said Human softly.

'Go and speak with two of my best scouts. Tell them they are to go to Earth and find out who these two blond women are who blew up my ship. I want to know who I am dealing with before I deliver my response to their insults! I want to know what I'm dealing with before I take Delavia *back*.' Valdazar spat.

Human felt sick and his heart raced in his chest. This could be a chance. His chance. His only chance. 'Ah, Sire, would you like me to go with the Scouts, just to make sure that the job is done correctly?

We do not want this to go wrong. Time is of the essence in devising our counter move to this attack on your Excellency. It is imperative that we get the honey pipeline up and running again for Anubis.'

Human held his breath and prayed to God that fate would shine in his favour.

Valdazar looked at Human as though he was seeing him for the first time. He was not used to Human being so proactive.

'Yes, yes I suppose. Those idiots get everything wrong. Yes, go with them and make sure they find those women. Ideally bring them both back here to me to answer for their crimes. They obviously have no idea who they are messing with! Bring them to me unharmed.'

Valdazars eyes shone with the thoughts of what he was going to do with the blonde woman and the young girl when he had them in his dungeon.

'Yes Sire, Right away.'

Human bowed to Valdazar and began walking out of the hall as fast as he could. As his legs moved so fast he was almost running, he felt hope soar in his chest. Now to find the two stupidest Valdons he could find he laughed inside.

He was on his way to find his Izzy. And there was NO WAY he would ever be coming back to this evil, abysmal place again.

Human felt lighter than he had in his entire life.

He was going *home*.

The Gathering of Inner Earth

Isadora could not be more embarrassed. She was literally sat in front of all these important looking people in her nighty. Just as she was cursing the gods, she felt her clothes change. She looked down in surprise to survey her body. She saw the ornate style of the Agarthans. She now had on a bright red pant suit with the Agarthan Fibonacci spiral insignia on. It fit like a dream. But how had she?

She looked up and surveyed the table. Directly to Isadora's right, Kaia beamed a huge, cat like grin at her.

'Kaia!' Exclaimed Isadora with glee. 'Thank you so much! You have no idea how embarrassed I was!' Isadora spoke telepathically into Kaia's head.

'Oh I had an idea,' teased Kaia. 'Given how red you went. But I couldn't hear your reaction as to my surprise, you have been working on your shield Isadora! I couldn't read you when you first got here! Well done!'

Isadora went red again. She had spent the last 4 weeks doing nothing but practice that white light shield to stop people accessing her mind without her permission. But she had no idea if she was getting any stronger, as she had no-one to practice on! Especially since she had not seen Chinga. She assumed that he'd been off looking for Peets but nobody had contacted her to tell her anything. Had Peets been found?

Isadora looked to her left and Orion. 'Orion, has Chinga found Peets?' She asked him hopefully. Orion's face changed and his smile fell. He looked down at the table.

'No not yet Ma'am,' the beautiful Cowboy said softly into her mind. 'It seems that when I closed the portal in such a hurry when we were escaping from Delavia, in haste, I ahhhh, I did something to it. It's malfunctioning. We've sent a few test people through it and each time it went somewhere else. Sometimes it works. But there's no consistency. Some people can still get in to Delavia. But some are going to totally different solar systems. And getting out of Delavia is a totally different ballgame if you don't have specialized equipment on you that tells you where you are when you hop. So unfortunately he could be anywhere in the entire Universe. If I hadn't have been in such a hurry, I probably would have done a much better job.' Orion looked like he was about to cry.

'Where is Chinga and his family?' Asked Isadora panicked. 'Is he OK?'
'He's doing OK under the circumstances Ma'am said Orion. He's with Lamay and Sneets and they're with one of our scouting parties who are out there looking for Peets. We have all available manpower out looking for him. We're doing everything we can. But as you can imagine,' said Orion sadly. 'It's like looking for a needle in a haystack. He could be anywhere. Anywhere at all. The Universe is vast. All we can do is keep looking and hope that we find him.'

Isadora stared into space. Chinga must be going out of his mind. She felt so sorry for her friend. She was missing him so very much. She wondered if there was anything she could do?
Suddenly silence fell around the huge oval table.

She looked again at the being who was seated at the far end of the long, oval table. Directly opposite her. It appeared that he was the one who was about to speak.

He had a humanoid body, but his face was very different. Apart from the fact that his skin was a beautiful shade of lilac, his nose was long and curled down his face like an elephant's trunk. He also had elephant like ears which were much bigger than any humans. Other than those two features which were very different, he looked much like the average human male.

'Thank you all for gathering here today for this emergency meeting,' said the unusual elephant looking man. His eyes met Isadora's. His eyes looked kind she thought. 'For the benefit of those of us who are new here, I will introduce everyone who sits around the table. To my right here is Babu, leader of the Amphibian clans.' The purple man gestured to the green looking lizard man. Babu nodded whilst staring at Isadora. 'Next to Babu is Pearl.' The purple man pointed to a beautiful black woman wearing an emerald green pantsuit. She had the most gorgeous mane of black curly hair cascading down her back and her eyes were accentuated with gold glitter. Streak of gold glitter ran through her jet black hair. She was stunning. 'Pearl is one of the founding families of the Mer People of Atlantis.'

Mer people of Atlantis? Thought Isadora excitedly. Atlantis, I've heard of that, but wasn't that destroyed? Suddenly Isadora had a bubble of excitement run up her spine. Mer people? Has she got a tail? I would love to be able to check under the table. Isadora slowly realised that the purple man had introduced the rest of the people around the table and she had not been listening! As colour ran up her cheeks she began to concentrate on what the purple man was saying.

'My name is Parmeethius,' he continued. ' I am a member of the Delo clan. The Delo clan are one of the original families to inhabit Inner Earth. We are gathered here today, each of the old Families of Inner Earth to discuss the emergency which has presented itself before us.' He glanced again at Isadora.

'Miss Stone, you have been summoned here today as a representative of the surface humans. So that when this meeting has been concluded, you may deliver a message to them from us.'

'A message?' Asked Isadora. 'What message, and to whom?' she asked bewilderedly.

'A message to your President from the Families of Inner Earth,' said Parmeethius looking intensely at the small blond teenager.

'The message is simply this,' he continued.

'STOP DIGGING NOW! STOP DIGGING RIGHT NOW! The Inner Earth is ours. It has always been ours. You have the surface. This is our home. It has been our home long before you surface humans came along. If you keep digging you are going to cause a War,' spat Parmeethius, beginning to lose his composure. And we will not have that. It is hard enough as it is to defend and maintain boundaries down here.'

'So the message is this,' he continued obviously trying to retain his countenance. 'Stop Digging now. Otherwise, the more ground you surface humans claim as your own, the more the Raptors will fight us to take our territory. We have managed, all of us, to maintain an equilibrium of sorts in Inner Earth for eons. We all have our own territories inside our beloved Gaia, and we do not encroach on another's ground. The Raptors are an evil race. A race of cruel, carnivorous beings who survived the meteor cataclysm of the Dinosaur ages by moving underground. They occupy the upper levels of the Inner Earth and we tolerate them as they have provided if you like, over the years, an element of protection for the Families of Inner Earth. The reason being that due to the ferocious nature of the Raptors, none of you surface humans have been able to make it down here to us, as you would have had to get past the Raptors first. The Raptors survive on the huge variety of animals that we have living down here. For example we have rats the size of dogs that live in Inner Earth,' Parmeethius explained.

'Lots of different animals live deep within the Earth that you surface humans have no idea about. There is also twice as much water inside the Earth as there is on the surface of the Earth. Living inside the Earth provides us with protection too. Protection from any meteorites or space debris that may strike the Earth. So we are very happy living deep within Gaia. However you surface humans are upsetting the equilibrium,' continued Parmeethius in a terse voice. 'You have been in recent times, boring down into the ground with huge boring tools and in so doing, you have disturbed the Raptor territory and they are not happy at all. They have lost huge quantities of hunting ground that used to belong to them. Your boring tools have disturbed and killed a lot of their normal food sources. In view of this, the Raptors have now started moving further down into the Earth in order to get away from your boring tools, but also in order to find more sources of food. After Eons of peace the Raptors are now fighting all of us old Inner Earth families in huge numbers, in order to take territory from us. This situation cannot continue. Soon if we do not stop this, it will escalate into out and out war, and we do not want to be at War with the Raptors. For the Raptors are friends with The Greys and we do not want to be at War with The Greys! For they also have other dark races of beings that they too are friends with and this will escalate very quickly. We have all of us, many races managed to exist peacefully within the Inner Earth of Gaia for Eons. The entire system works. And now you surface humans have upset that equilibrium,' said Parmeethius looking directly at Isadora. 'This cannot happen. We cannot have war within the Earth. Because if there is war within the Earth, it will spill up and out onto the surface of Gaia. And then you surface humans will become involved whether you like it or not.'

'War!' Whispered Isadora shocked. 'And I have to take this message to the President?'

'Yes, and you need to do it today,' concluded Parmeethius sternly. 'After this meeting. There is no time to lose. Even now the surface humans are digging. Even now the Raptors are looking to regain back the ground they have lost by moving further within and into our territory. You must go to your President today and insist that this stops right now. Unless the President wants war within his own world as a result. For we Delo will not stand idly by whilst our way of life is taken from us.'

Excellent. Thought Isadora coming to terms with this twist of events. The last time I saw the President I had to tell him about General Myers blowing up the Valdons and Valdazar. I also had to tell him that Earth was endangered due to the levels of negativity and that the food chain was starting to be effected. As a result the President had promised Isadora that he would look into an initiative that would provide some protection for the bees. He had also promised that he would look into what she had told him about the negativity on Earth. And now this.

'He's going to love me.' She thought as she stared at the curious, elephant faced man.

'OK, tell me what I need to do.' Isadora sighed.

Chinga

Chinga was trying really hard to stay strong for Lamay and Sneets. But panic was constantly in his heart, chest and mind. Where is my Son, he screamed internally.

He had this same question going through his mind all the time. Day after day. When he woke up, when he went to sleep. 'Where is my Son? Where is my Peets?'

He had been devastated when he had found out that the portal on Delavia was not working properly. He remembered that Orion had done something to it as they had left Delavia in a hurry, but he had no idea the consequences that this would cause within his own life. Within his own family. The guilt of this knawed away at him. It was constantly there sat hand in hand with his nerves. Waiting at any moment to cause his temper to flare. His own guilt at failing his Son made him snappy and fretful. If only he had not gone to the honey planet. It was just honey. They did not need it to survive. They just *wanted* it. He had no idea that Peets had watched him go through the portal. That Peets knew where the portal was. He rubbed his head painfully as he thought about his Son leaving Delavia in search of him. He had thought he was going to Earth. But the portal was not aligned to go to Earth at that time. And it seemed that it wasn't working properly anyway! Peets of course had not known this. They had checked all the magnetic alignment maps that Orion had access to. The portal had been aligned at the exact time that Peets had gone through it, to a planet called Quential. Quential was where they were now sat. Where they had been for the past 4 weeks since this whole nightmare had unfolded. For the past 4 weeks they had searched this planet high and low. Every person they had come across, Chinga had pleaded with. 'Have you seen my Son?' with hope in his eyes. But nothing. Peets was not here. Peets was not here. He felt it in his heart.

And he knew it. As he could not connect to his Son telepathically. Peets was not on Quential. So where was he?

Chinga looked at Lamay and Sneets who had fallen asleep together next to the campfire that they had built together and tears rolled down the soft orangey brown fur of his face. He loved his family so very much. They meant everything to him. They were what his heart beat for. It was his role to protect them. And he had let them down. There was only one last place to try, and that was with the Elders who governed this planet. Tomorrow they would start their trek up the mountains to the place where these founding beings of Quential lived. Since their scouting party had been here they had met many people. Quential was beautiful. Almost as beautiful as Delavia Chinga considered. The people were humanoid and looked much like the humans of Earth. But they were different. They were *peaceful.* They had different powers to the ones from Earth. Some of them could fly. Some of them could move objects with their minds. They were all happy. They lived in wonderful communities in nature, where they all helped each other and looked after each other. Their children looked so happy. The light shone out of them. Chinga watched a group of Quential children laughing with each other and playing whilst their parents looked happily on, relaxed. If my boy is here, he will be OK Chinga thought. But where IS he?

Chinga sobbed quietly as he looked up into the night sky and searched the stars for answers.

'Where is my boy!' he screamed inside as his eyes scanned the sky for a sign. Some sign of hope.

'Where is my Son?'

Earth

Human could not believe this was happening. He could not believe his luck. He could not believe that his master had let him go! Why? Why had Valdazar agreed to this? Normally he insists that I go with him everywhere, Human considered. So why has he let me go?

He's reeling from the attack on Delavia, Human thought. It had completely surprised him. No-one had challenged him for a very long time. He knew this had really affected his Master as he had witnessed the terse conversation between Valdazar and Anubis. Valdazar had had to eat humble pie and explain that Delavia had been taken back. This was something that Valdazar had not been expecting at all! Thus far, Human had not seen *anyone* stand up to his Master. But he had only been with him for four years. It had made him so happy to see Valdazar having to explain to Anubis that his next installment of honey would be delayed as there was a 'situation'. It had made him look weak. And this had pleased Anubis immensely. Although Anubis never showed how he felt to Valdazar. Anubis despised him. He hated having to deal with him but it was a necessary evil as Valdazar seemed to have his tentacles in everything. Which was baffling as he had only been on the scene for a very short time in terms of the longevity of the Cosmos. But in the 29 years that Valdazar had led the Valdons, he had systematically conquered their entire Galaxy.

Human contemplated his master. He was so scared of him. But why? Because he's a psychopath that's why! He thought. He recalled the scene in his mind when he had first been brought before his new 'master' and had seen Valdazar for the first time. After being captured by the two scout Valdons and spending around a day on their ship. He remembered being brought before 'him' on his throne. His throne had looked like a dragon. Serantium, Human thought, what a strange material. It had glistened like silver. A menacing silver dragon. But he quickly realised that the dragon was not real. As his eyes had looked up in fear at this huge dragon, he had seen his new 'Master' sat on top of the dragon's head. On first glance, Human had thought, 'this is who everyone is scared of?' He looks like a skinny mad man with a black beard. As he peered up at his new master he saw that 'Valdazar' appeared to be in his late 30's. He was clad in a black leather outfit peppered with huge angry looking spikes. These spikes were all over Valdazars outfit in various shapes and sizes with the longest glistening menacingly above his neck. Valdazar was waving at him on the back of this gigantic metal looking dragon and laughing. He had some sort of stick in his hand and looked like he was conducting an orchestra. Surely this was not who the Valdons worshipped? He looked pale, unhealthy and skinny as a rake. But quite happy? Albeit in a deranged sort of way. Humans' spirits had started to lift, maybe things were not so bad? Maybe he could negotiate his way out of this. The Valdons had drugged him on the journey to this new place, but the drugs were starting to lift. He was sure he could 'take' this guy. He didn't look too heavy. And they were a similar age. The Valdons were enormous. But maybe he could negotiate with them too. Human reeled as the memory of his arriving at Valdar came back so clearly. He carried on allowing the memory to resurface as he strode off to find two Valdons to make the journey to Earth. The memory continued as he hurriedly paced, excitedly on his quest back home. He remembered that when he had been captured Valdazar had slowly hovered down to where he was stood and strode off the neck of the metallic dragon. The two of them had stood eye to eye. It was at that point that Valdazar had pierced him for the first time, with the stick that he held in his hand. Human had not seen it coming. The stick took him to his knees with a pain that he had never experienced before. Whatever that stick was – it was pure evil. He had thought he could negotiate his way out of this misunderstanding and get home to his wife and daughter who were making brownies. But as he had stood face to face with Valdazar. He realised quickly that he had underestimated him. This man was pure darkness and worse than that, he was insane. It didn't matter that Valdazar was skinny and didn't look like he had an ounce of muscle on him. An evil energy drove him. Human had never met anyone like that before. Not on Earth. This man had no compassion. There was no reasoning with him. As Valdazar had struck Human again with this spike that contained a technology that he did not understand, excruciating pain had coursed throughout Humans body. That was the start of his training. When Human first arrived at Valdar, his new Master would spike him with this excruciatingly painful stick over and over again. Until Human would do anything that Valdazar wanted. Anything. To not be taken to that dark place of pain again. Before he was captured by the Valdons he was Oliver. That was his name. Husband to Catherine Stone. Father to Isadora Stone. After weeks of being with Valdazar and being tortured hourly, he became 'Human'.

New fear coursed through Humans body. *Why did he let me go so easily*, he thought?

Then he realised. Valdazar had let him go as he was desperate to regain control of the situation that he had found himself in. He wasn't thinking straight. He is a *psychopath*. And for once – he feels out of control. So he's let me go, Human's thoughts raced. And in doing so, he has made a fatal mistake thought Human happily, as now I am on my way back to my daughter and my beautiful wife.

Human walked into the great hall and deliberately picked the two stupidest Valdons that he was aware of. *'Master needs some work doing'* was all he said as he gestured to Greb and Than. The two giants gingerly got up and followed Human out of the hall. They knew that Human was involved in all of Valdazars most important schemes and never questioned Humans direction. Greb and Than were two of the physically weakest Valdons that lived on Valdar. They were the runts of the pack if you like. They didn't question anything. They just went along with it. As Human led the two stupid brutes out of the great hall, he had a brief wave of fear engulf him. Valdazar would be furious when he found out *who* he had taken. But by then I will be long gone thought Human. Thoughts of his daughter and wife gave him the necessary strength to take the action he was about to take.

He had not had much time to devise a plan. But thus far, his plan in his mind looked like this. Take the two stupidest and weakest Valdons with him to Earth. Learn how to fly the scout ship on the way to Earth. He so wished he had paid more attention to this prior to now! He would collect his wife and daughter first and tell the Valdons that they would then pick up the blonde woman. Or maybe he could convince Greb and Than that his wife *was* the blonde woman? I'll somehow have to not alert Catherine and Izzy to the fact that it is me though as they will give the game away and the Valdons will wonder how they know me? Human nervously considered this. How could he disguise himself? I will cover my face with something.....but what? Once his daughter and wife were located and in the scout ship. Then he somehow had to outmaneuver the Valdons and get them out of the craft and take off without them. He thought about how he could do this. He could encourage them to pick up some cows. They seemed to love eating cows. There were cows throughout their Galaxy. They loved eating any and all large animals and there were many large animals in the Universe. Whilst the Valdons were distracted by hunting their next meal. Isadora, his wife and himself could take off. He would have to be quick as when the Valdons realised what had happened they would alert their master through their chest plates. What they did after that he wasn't sure. They would have to find somewhere to hide. But that wasn't a problem. The Universe was a big place. And Human was used to making himself disappear into the shadows. Human had not felt as happy in a long time. He was on his way to pick up his wife and daughter. He was on his way to freedom.

The President

Isadora was currently on her way down to the ship hangar bay in Agartha City. She had not realised at first that it was Agartha City they were in, as the room the meeting had been held in was very big and very grand indeed. It was a gigantic cavern, and unfamiliar to her from her previous visit to Agartha. This huge cavern was situated right near the great hall of Agartha. And once again she marveled at the beauty of this magical place. As they left the cavern of the meeting and strode into the main City of Agartha. Isadora drank in the beauty of their world. Exotic birds flew above huge expanses of crops. Lush trees and streams peppered the horizon. In the main square, the Agarthans wandered around happily conversing with each other. Silver disk spacecrafts zipped around in the air and through the cavern wall as people left and arrived. Isadora remembered a previous conversation with Adama where he had explained that the food that the Agarthans grew was prized around the Cosmos for its quality and flavor. The Agarthans traded some of their food for additional resources that they needed here. Isadora could see people in the fields loading crops onto a small silver spaceship. Isadora wondered where the source of light came from in this place and scanned the scenery. Way off in the distance, she could see a large glimmering ball of white light, which looked very much like a small sun. Interesting.

Her thoughts returned to where they were going. Shortly after the meeting had finished, Orion and Kaia had explained that it was them who would be taking her to see the President and that they would in fact be making their way down to the ship hangar bay now.

Her heart did flip flops as she thought about Adama. Not one day had gone by in the 4 weeks that she had not seen him that she had not thought about him. She thought about him all the time. She had told herself that she would likely never see him again. But this did not matter. For a very small window of time, he had been hers. And she held onto that very tightly. She had held onto the image of him in her mind so many times. And whilst his image was starting to fade a bit now. She still remembered his gorgeous dark curly hair which he tucked behind his ears. And his smile. He had a dazzling smile.

And now she was in Agartha City! But they were leaving! Would she get to see him she wondered? She hoped.

'Ah, Kaia,' she asked trying to sound nonchalant as she enquired about her love interest. 'How is everyone? Is Tiamut OK after what happened on Delavia? Is Adama OK too?'

'Ah Isadora,' smiled Kaia as she walked with purpose towards the Ship Hangar Bay Room. 'I wondered when you might enquire about the lovely Adama!' Kaia's eyes danced.

Isadora blushed beetroot red and looked at her toes as she walked to the ship.

'Your friend Adama is fine and has requested that he might see you if possible when we return from our mission. I assume that will be agreeable to yourself?' Kaia smiled.

'Yes of course, I mean that would be great. It would be lovely to see him.' Mumbled Isadora as pure panic rushed through her mind. What would she say to him? Thank god she wasn't still wearing her nighty! 'I'm sure if all goes well with the President tonight, we will have time to return here for a bit so you can have a catch up with Adama. Before we return you to your room in time for morning. We don't want your Momma to be worried about where you have gone to now do we?' Kaia laughed as she started walking up into one of the smaller ships in the hangar bay.

'Follow me!' She confirmed and disappeared into the small ship.
Orion who had been quiet on route to the ship, presumably still lost in thought about Chinga and Peets, said 'After you Ma-am' and gestured for Isadora to go first.

She smiled at Orion and began to climb into the ship.

Here we go again she thought as excitement coursed through her veins. It's the middle of the night and I'm on my way to go see the President of the United States in a spaceship with an Inner Earth being and a Cowboy Alien.

This was almost starting to feel 'normal.'

David

David was currently sat in the Medical bay on a white bed trying to work out what had just happened. Nathan had stopped him from getting to Peets, he remembered that much. Nathan had hit him, a lot. His body should be black and blue. He knew he had lost consciousness and he had tasted blood in his mouth and felt the hot liquid stream down his face when Nathan had broken his nose. But he wasn't black and blue. He didn't hurt anywhere. He felt great!
But that doesn't make sense David thought. Why don't I have any injuries?

When he had regained consciousness, he had been looking into the eyes of a dark haired girl. He had seen her before. She was always on her own. She never seemed to mix with anybody. David didn't think he had ever seen her with any family. He remembered her for that exact reason. The fact that she was always on her own. And the fact that she always looked sad. As he had reminded himself how grateful he was that he had his Mother and Father. That he too wasn't on his own. And now he was. Just like the dark haired girl.

He wiped the back of his hand over his face to smear away the hot tears. Who was that girl and what had she done to him? All he could remember was that when he came round, she was holding him. And her embrace had felt incredible. Like she had filled him up with light. Like she had put him back together again. It had felt like an energy coming from her to him. Like electricity. Like pure happiness.

David wondered who the girl was. He focused his mind on when he had first seen her. She had just appeared there one day. He had seen her at the breakfast gathering one morning. Nothing ever really happened there so if there was anyone new, it was always a form of excitement to the people kept captive there. Where had the new person come from? Had they come from Earth? Was Earth still OK?

Did they have any news? If someone new had arrived then that meant new people were still being brought in. Which in turn could mean that there was a way out and off this planet if they could just figure out how. He had remembered that several of the more brave members of the group had tried to speak with the new girl, to find out where she was from. But no-one could get her to talk. She just shook her head and looked down. In the end, everyone had just thought she was too traumatized by whatever events had brought her there, and people just left her alone. And she never sought anyone's company. So who was she? And why had she helped him? And *how* had she healed him? David thought about Peets and the task ahead. He was supposed to be getting as much information to Peets as possible about the compound inside and the guards. Weapons. Systems inside. When Eldon was there and when he wasn't, as they would break free on a day when he wasn't there. How everything worked. This dark haired girl could be a useful asset to David in helping collect this information. He wanted to help Peets and his friends, so Peets could help all of them escape. And when the time was right, Peets and his friends would help break them all out. Then God help all of the guards who had kept them captive here on Mars. God help them. As once his people had a taste of freedom again, they would never go back in a cage again.

David needed to make friends with this girl.

He felt it was his destiny.

Peets

Peets had waited until the humans had all filed in from their break and the portly guard had ambled back inside. All was now deserted back at the exercise yard and eerily quiet.

Peets slowly got up off the hard red desert floor and stretched out his aching limbs. What did he do now he thought?

I have to go back and tell Koro what has happened. David had looked like he had taking a really bad beating and had fallen unconscious. But then the dark haired girl had done something to David. And David had woken up. Who was this dark haired girl? He wondered if David knew her?

Would this set their plan back? Would David be OK? Peets began to worry as he started to hurry back to the caves. If David was injured it might take a long time for him to get the information that we need. Mother and Sneets will be so worried about me by now. And what about Father I wonder if he has returned from the Honey planet yet? Fear started to wash over him in waves. What would they do now? What happens if they couldn't free the incarcerated humans? Would The Cockroaches and Mantis still let him use the portal map and the portal? Would he ever get home? Peets started to cry and he increased his fast walk to a run. He ran and ran and ran as fast as his little legs would carry him back up to the caves.

By the time he burst into Koro's cave, Peets was sobbing.
'What happened my child?' said Koro, the large, wise Bear.
'It all went wrong, it all went wrong!' Cried Peets, his chest heaving.
'David was on his way over to me and then 3 boys stopped him and they hit him over and over and knocked him to the floor.'
Koro frowned, 'Go on, then what happened?' Said the Bear urgently.
'Then this dark haired girl came up and said something to the boys and they left! And then she got down on the floor with David and held

him. Almost like she was hugging him. And then he woke up and he seemed fine? But the guards came in and they took him away! Oh Koro cried the young Sasquatch, I hope David is OK? What happens if he doesn't come back? What if I don't see him again? The Cockroaches will not let me see the map and the Mantis won't let me use the portal and I will never get home. I'm *never* going to see my family again!' the little Sasquatch sank to his knees and sobbed.

Koro walked slowly to the little orange brown ball of fur sobbing on his cave floor. He placed a large soft paw on his heaving back.

'My child, I promise you I will do everything in my power to get you back to your family. All is not lost. Sometimes things happen that were not 'to plan.' But often these things have a way of being for our highest good. A dark haired girl hugged him you say? And then he seemed fine?'

'Yes,' confirmed Peets. 'She pulled him to her and hugged him and then his eyes opened and he seemed to be OK again.'

'Interesting,' whispered the Bear. 'Tomorrow you will go back to the same place and watch for David and for this dark haired girl. If David does not come back out. See if you can attract the attention of the girl instead. She may be able to get a message to David. All is not lost little one. There are setbacks in every mission. It is to be expected. But maybe, just maybe this was meant to happen for a reason.'

Peets wiped his nose on the back of his furry arm and looked up at the gigantic Bear. 'What are you thinking Koro?' he sniffed.

'I'm thinking that maybe there is something special about this dark haired girl that you speak of. And maybe what happened today was necessary to bring David and this girl together. The creator works in mysterious ways. This girl could be useful to David. And it sounds like David could use a new friend.'

Peets rubbed his face and started to feel brighter. Koro always had a way of making him feel better.

'Yes you are right. I will go back tomorrow and try again. All is not lost. I *will* get back home to my family. And I will help to free those humans.'

'That's better my child,' smiled the kind Bear. 'We will get you home.'

The White House

Isadora, Orion and Kaia sat in the Agarthan spaceship. This ship was one of the smallest Isadora had seen in the hangar bay. A small silver disk. It was large enough to fit three tall humans inside with a bit of room to spare.

'Ah Kaia,' asked Isadora. 'Are we going to let the President know that we are coming? We don't just want to 'turn up' at the Whitehouse in this thing! What happens if they shoot us?' She laughed nervously. The last time she had met with the President, he had sent a car to collect her. And she had been driven to the Whitehouse. She wasn't sure how the President would take to them turning up in a spaceship.

'I am glad you have mentioned that Isadora,' Kaia smiled. 'As you already have a 'relationship' with the President, we think he will respond better to this meeting if you contact him first and inform us of our journey.'

'OK....and you want me to do that....how?' Isadora asked baffled. 'It's not like I have his private number or anything! She laughed nervously. I met him like once! He's probably forgotten who I am by now! He's the President of the United States!'

Orion opened a pocket on his dazzling chaps and brought out the Smart Glass pad that she had seen on their very first meeting. Orion had been taking her to Area 51 to meet Chinga and he had used the Smart Glass pad to show Isadora her Mother.

'Did y'all forget about this Isadora? Orion's special toy! He laughed. 'Remember what you do. You hold it in your hand and think about who you want to see and then you'll be able to speak to him.'

'How will I be able to speak to The President Orion? Doesn't he have to have one too? When you showed me my Momma that time, I just 'saw' her in the pad, I didn't speak to her? How do I speak to him?'

'The President has one of these things on his desk Isadora,' Orion smiled.' He currently thinks it's a fancy cup holder or something. He's about to be educated otherwise,' Orion winked.

'How do you know all this Orion?' laughed Isadora. 'How do you know so much about the President?'

'Ma'am, I work at Area 51 for a branch of the United States Government. This branch of Government has been historically operating outside of the awareness of the office of the President. The President has generally been kept on a 'need to know basis.' And the branch of the government that I work for has in the past decided that the President does not need to know much. Do you understand what I'm saying?' He drawled.

'The President has been kept in the dark?' Isadora guessed.

'That is correct Ma'am. However *this* President that we have right now. He's different from the others before him. He's been asking questions. He wants to know more about what's going on in the various factions of government that has otherwise been hidden from that position of office. Since he met with you after we got back from Delavia, he has been requesting more and more information about what the various branches of government are studying. He's made enquiries about our friends The Greys and their base. He's also made enquiries about our lovely friend Kaia here and her people the Agarthans. *This* President is different. The others before him have not been interested in the larger workings of the different branches of operations. This President seems to genuinely care. It has been noted. We made sure he had one of these pads on his desk for some time now,' Orion said pointing to the Smart Glass pad. 'As we had a feeling that we would be needing to contact him directly soon. Through this pad, we can get straight to him and cut out the middle guys. He has not been shown how to work it yet. He thinks it's just a piece of Perspex on his desk. I think he's been using it as a cup holder,' Orion laughed.

'Ah OK,' smiled Isadora, 'well he's going to get a shock when I contact him on his 'cup holder' then isn't he?' Oh boy, she thought. How do I get myself into these situations?

'Now remember what you do Isadora,' guided Orion. 'You put the pad in your hand and you think of the President. But this time, 'think' that you want to make *contact* with him. This will trigger his Smart Glass pad to come on and away we go!'

'I can't believe I'm doing this,' said Isadora nervously. 'OK, here we go.'

Isadora took the pad from Orion and thought about the President. She could picture him in her mind's eye. He was a kind man with a huge genuine smile and blond hair. He was in his 70's but you wouldn't believe it. He looked great for his age. She 'thought' about making contact with the President. The Smart Glass pad changed from being clear Perspex and started to swirl. As the swirling fog cleared Isadora stared straight up the Presidents nose as he drank a cup of coffee and placed it back down over his Smart Glass pad obscuring her view.

'Ah Mr President.....Sir,' Isadora said gingerly, trying hard not to laugh at the President using his advanced technology as a coffee mat. 'It's Isadora Stone Sir.'

'Jeeeeeesus' jumped the President, 'what the........? What is that thing? I thought it was a darn drinks holder. Scared me half to.......'

The President ran his hand through his hair and adjusted his tie. He removed the coffee cup so he could see who or what was talking to him.

He squinted at the mat. 'Isadora....is that you?' The President laughed. 'What is this thing on my desk? I thought it was a darn coffee holder? I've been using it for my drink!' He laughed. 'Did you leave this here when you came to see me?' the President winked.

'Ah no Sir, I didn't leave it.' Isadora's voice trailed off. 'Sir would you mind picking it up and placing it on your hand so we can see you properly.' Isadora did not want to have to explain to the President of the United States that she could see straight up his nose.

'Errr sure,' said the President trying to get his head round this new development. 'Just a second.' He picked up the pad and it started to mold into a more comfortable shape in his hand.

'What is this thing?' Laughed the President and how am I able to see you on it?'

'It's a Smart Glass pad Sir, I'm told that it's very advanced technology. Sir, the reason I am disturbing you at this late hour, and I apologise for that, is we have a problem that I need to come and speak with you about.'

The President rubbed his eyes with his unobscured hand. What time was it? Once again he was working late in his office trying to get a handle on everything that was happening in his country.

'A problem? How can I help you Isadora?' Said the President as he started to think about their last meeting. This 15 year old American schoolgirl had helped save another planet from being taken over by a guy called Valdazar who he was told, was a mad conqueror who went around his own Galaxy and one by one enslaved everyone. Now apparently he had tried to start taking over the Milky Way. But this sweet girl and her friends who were Sasquatch and tall humans who lived inside Earth had blown this Valdazar guy to smithereens. Well it wasn't them. It was some rogue faction of *his* government. One that up until meeting Isadora and hearing her story, he had been entirely unaware of. Since that meeting with Isadora 4 weeks ago. He had steadily been making enquiries with regards to the *shady* arms of the government that he had otherwise been kept in the dark about. It was his responsibility as the President of the United States to keep his people safe. How could he keep the American people safe if so much information was kept away from him? He needed to know everything. And he needed to get a handle on these 'dark operations' that had seemed to operate under the radar of previous Presidents before him. He did not understand why that had happened. He only knew that it stopped with him. He would not rest until he had unpicked it all and he was aware of everything.

When he had first met Isadora he could not believe the story she had told him. Apparently this Valdazar guy was Human and originally came from Earth? How the hell had he ended up on another planet? But as he listened to her recounting everything she had experienced, he knew she was telling the truth. There was an honesty about this girl that was so genuine. She seemed very special. Apparently she could communicate with people telepathically! Now there was a skill! After their meeting he had set about finding out as much as he could about all of the things that had previously been hidden from him. It seems that even the President of the United States is only told things on a 'need to know' basis too. And he was told that much of what really went on. He didn't 'need' to know.

'Well' began Isadora, 'I was at home tonight Sir in bed, and then the next minute I was portalled into Agartha City. You know the place I told you about Sir, inside the Earth that's like a paradise?'

'With the tall humans?' the President asked?

'Yes Sir, I have one of them here with me at the moment. Kaia. She is a priestess here in Agartha City. And I also have Orion with me too Sir.'

'Orion – he's the Cowboy Alien right? From Alpha Centauri?'

'Yes Sir that is correct.'

Orion laughed 'Hoo hoo, God damn President knows who Orion is alright!' he cried.

'Ah yes, thanks Orion,' said Isadora embarrassed. 'Sir, I was brought to a Council meeting where there were different races of beings there that all live under the Earth in different places other than Agartha. There was one being there called Parmeethius who was a member of the Delo clan.' Isadora paused for breath.

'Delo clan you say?' Frowned the President. 'Who are they?'

'I believe they are a race of beings who live inside the Earth Sir and have done for millions of years and…. they have faces that look a bit like an elephant. And they are purple.'

The President rubbed his face again. Purple Elephants. Of course.

'OK Isadora, I think it would be better if we have this discussion face to face. I can send a car for you in the morning if you like? 9.00am sharp?'

'Sir, we're actually in a spaceship right now and well, we could come now to you. If you would like.' Isadora felt so embarrassed.

The President sat back in his chair and stared at the serious blond haired teenager.

'You are in a spaceship and you can come here now?' he said incredulously. 'What like you can fly over America and land on the White House lawn?'

'If I may interject,' said Kaia with a smile. 'Could you tell the President that there is a portal located in the White House Rose Garden? If he would be so kind as to send someone out to escort us to him. We can be there in 10 minutes. I will keep the ship cloaked so no-one will see us arrive. I am sure the President would prefer discretion.'

'Ah did you hear all that Sir,' said Isadora nervously?

'10 minutes hey?' Said the President rubbing his face incredulously. 'Sure I'll send someone down to meet you and escort you up. The Rose Garden you say? They will be carrying guns but please do not be alarmed. This is standard protocol for the Whitehouse.'

'OK Sir, thank you. We will see you in 10 minutes!' Said Isadora brightly and the image of Isadora Stone's face slowly faded away.

The President sat back in his chair and ran his hands through his hair.

'There's a portal in the goddam Rose Garden?...Purple Elephants?'

The Journey to Earth

Human sat in the small Valdon Scout ship and watched intently as Greb and Than flew the disk. It did not seem to be so difficult, he thought. All they did was put their huge hands on the silver steering plates of the ships and the ship reacted to their touch and moved.

Human was not sure how they did this. Did they do this with their minds? As the Valdons could not speak telepathically. He doubted sometimes that they even had minds given how they conducted themselves. He sat silently behind them and watched them navigate the small ship. The huge brutes put their hands on the silver plates and the ship moved. They didn't both need to put their hands on the plates at the same time, Human noted, for the ship to move. Would *his* hands work on this ship given that his hands were smaller?

Greb had his hands on the plates and Than was studying some star maps that were currently on the big screen in front of them.

'Where we goin?' slurred Than to Human.

'Earth in the Milky Way Galaxy.' Said Human quietly.

Than grunted and started swiping the screen until he had the necessary star map in fr'ont of him.

'How do we get there? Asked Human gingerly. 'Are we using the portal system?'

'Yeah,' bellowed Than. 'We got to go to a few stops first before we get there.' Than squinted at the star map on the screen. 'It ses ere that we get to Earth through using portals to Bazantire first, then jump to Quential, then we get to a portal above the Moon of Earth. Then we can portal into Earth through the ocean and come up there. Take about 5 days to jump these portals. Did you tell the Master?' Than asked with a worried expression on his ugly face.

'Yes,' answered Human quickly. 'Master knows.'

Human sat and contemplated what that meant. Valdazar would be pacing up and down for 5 days wondering what had happened. He would no doubt try to contact them on the ships technology. But by then they would have put considerable space between him and his master. Human would manage his expectations. He would contact Valdazar often and keep him sweet. Stop him from doing anything rash. I have 5 days to learn how to fly this thing and to formulate my plan of escape he thought. Nothing would stop him getting back to his family. Nothing.

The Dark Haired Girl

David had been checked over by the medi bay staff and released into the population. Some of the staff in the medi bay were very old. They were the original people who had come from Earth who themselves were incarcerated by Eldon. Lied to. Some of the younger Doctors had been children when they had left Earth and were trained in medicine by the original Doctors who had been brought here on the ships. David had only been treated with kindness in the medi bay. He could tell they had prolonged his stay as long as possible. They had given him food. But having found nothing wrong, he was released back into the normal population.

   A kindly doctor walked him back down to the canteen room. A younger doctor, around 40 years old with love in her face, despite the conditions. 'Best of luck to you David,' she smiled as she led him into the canteen. 'Stay away from Nathan and his friends now' she smiled with love and weariness in her face.

   David smiled at her and looked at the canteen room. Everyone was busy queuing up for their food or already eating. They did not see the small boy enter.

 David quickly scanned the room. Where was she? Suddenly he saw the dark haired girl leaving the end of the queue for food and sitting at a table on her own. Always on her own.

 David kept his head down and scurried over to her table. Everyone was so preoccupied with either eating or queuing for food that no-one noticed him enter back into the population.

   David sat down in front of the dark haired girl.

The girl looked up. No-one ever sat with her. Upon seeing it was David, a huge smile burst upon her face. David noticed for the first time that the girl was in fact very beautiful. She quickly searched him for marks. And then upon realising her mistake. She hurriedly looked down again and resumed pushing her food around her plate.

'Thank you,' said David quietly, 'for what you did for me today. My name is David. And.....I could do with a friend....like you in here.'
The dark haired girl carried on pushing food around her plate.
'Who are you?' Asked David. 'And why did you help me?'
The dark haired girl looked up once quickly and scanned the room. She looked back down at her plate.
David thought that the girl would never speak. But it didn't matter. He was happy that he was just sat here with her. He wasn't hungry as they had given him food in the medi bay. He was just grateful to be sat with someone in this place who had showed him compassion.
Suddenly David heard a voice in his head.
'My name is Aurora,' the sweet voice said. I come from the planet Quential. They brought me here as I have special powers and they are using me to help them create new technology. As I can see in to the future. I can see what will work and what will not work. I do not want to be here. I was taken from my people. From my planet. My home is beautiful.'
David reeled as the dark haired girl placed images in his head of her planet. It was the most beautiful place that he had ever seen. So much beauty. Lush trees and vibrant flowers. Expanses of what looked like lakes and children playing and laughing, splashing each other in the water. Sunrises and sunsets. Water lapping up onto the land above. Harmony and Peace. David had never seen anything like it before in his 8 years on this harsh planet.
David began to cry, huge tears ran down his face and he put his head down so no-one could see. He felt the feeling of love which he had experienced with his parents but magnified a thousand times.
'Yes, David, Yes,' said the dark haired girl into David's mind. I have experienced wonders on my planet that you would never believe are real. Quential is beautiful. My people are so happy. THEY came one

night in their big ships and they took me. They want what we have on Quential. But they can never obtain it as they do not have love in their cold hearts. They cannot obtain the *powers* of Quential, because to live in that power you have to operate from your heart. These cruel beings do not. They do not operate from their hearts. All they know is cruelty and oppression. They took *me* as they were angry. They took me as they wanted our power. And I *was* someone very powerful on my planet. Not powerful as they see. But powerful there. I was the Keeper of the Crystal on Quential. I harnessed the power of the Crystal across all of the Universe and I harnessed it for the good of my people. I used the power of the Crystal to keep my people healthy. Our planet is so full of power. Power from the one true creator as we respect the power of the One. We respect the power of the all. We respect each other. We love each other. These humans who have captured us here. They do not respect life. They do not even respect each other. They have brought me here to hurt my planet. As without me there to read the Crystal and channel the healing powers, my people will be weakened.'

David sat with his head down listening to everything that this strange girl was placing into his head. How was she able to access his mind? He felt so sorry for her. She was feeling the loss of her home and family. And he was too. His thoughts darted to his parents again. He missed them so much. We're they still alive? Why had Eldon's men taken them?

'Your parents are still alive my friend.' Said the dark haired girl into David's mind. 'I work with them daily. He is keeping them in a separate room underground. Eldon feels that if he separates them from you then he will get them to do what he wants quicker. They were stalling. He knew. They don't want to do what Eldon wants them to do. And so he has separated them from you so he can tell your parents that if they don't do what he says, he will harm you.'

David's head shot up bolt right and he looked at the girl. Her head was still down and she was still pushing her food around her plate.

'My parents are alive?' he said out loud.

'Shhhhhh,' she said directly into David's head.

David put his head down and looked at the table. Elation coursed through his fragile frame. 'Please,' he said in his head, 'tell me what you know about my parents!'

'He keeps them in one of the underground rooms, further down than ours. He doesn't want you to know that they are still alive. Your parents have been working on a weapon. A weapon that Eldon wants in order to gain dominion over this part of the Galaxy in total. Your parents were stalling. They knew what their science would bring. And they were delaying in giving him the final scientific figures. That's why he took them.'

'My parents are alive!' David shouted in his head. 'My parents are alive!' He quickly scanned the canteen room and everyone was still eating their food and looking down. Speaking in hushed whispers.

'Yes my friend,' said the dark haired girl into David's excited head. 'Your parents are alive. And I am brought to them daily. They are aware of my powers and are trying to get me to see if their *science* will work.'

'Can you tell them that I am OK?' Thought David happier than he had ever been. His heart soared. His parents were *alive*!' Can you tell them that I know that they are alive and I'm working on a plan to get us out of here? Can you tell them that I love them so much?' Emotion filled the little boy's chest and his eyes swam with tears of joy.

Suddenly the dark haired girl looked up at David. She still did not speak with her mouth. Only her mind. Again her voice entered David's head.

'You are working on a plan to get us out of here?'

'Yes,' thought David. 'I have a friend called Peets who has made it onto this planet by accident. He is a little orange Sasquatch. I met him at the back of the exercise pen one day when my parents had just been taken. I was praying to God for a miracle as I just did not want to live anymore now they had taken my parents from me. I thought Eldon had killed them. I thought I was alone. I was so scared. I felt there was no reason for me to be alive anymore if my parents were gone. And I didn't want to live here without them. I prayed for a miracle or a sign from God that everything was going to be OK. And then as if by magic, Peets began speaking to me from the sandy floor. His fur blends into the colour of the sand here and I hadn't seen him,' said David excitedly. 'Peets wants to go home to his planet called Delavia. In order to get access to the portal map from the Cockroaches, so he knows when to travel back through the portal system. He has agreed to help the Cockroaches take this facility back from Eldon. Apparently according to Peets the Cockroaches and the Bears and the Mantis *hate* Eldon. Like really hate him. They feel that he has taken over their planet. And they want it back. Especially the Mantis as they control the portal that is in the Lava tubes. When Eldon first arrived on this planet 35 years ago they tried to take the Lava tubes from the Mantis as Eldon knew that there was a portal in there. They wanted to control the whole planet and they could only do this if they had control of all the portals on here. Peets said there was a huge battle between the Mantis and Eldon's army and Eldon's army was defeated and had to retreat. Since then Eldon has maintained control of the other portal that is apparently off in the desert on the surface of the planet, but the Mantis still have control of the portal in the Lava tubes. That is the one that we can escape from,' said David excitedly. 'The Bears, Cockroaches and Mantis are willing to help us break out if it means getting control of this facility back from Eldon. And in return for Peets helping them get control of this facility, the Cockroaches will then let Peets see the portal map, and then he will be able to get back to his home planet. Peets told me all I have to do is get as much information as possible to him about the guards and what happens inside the facility so he and the Bears and Cockroaches can formulate a plan to break us all out! I was going to meet Peets the day that you saved me from Nathan. All I need to do is give Peets the information he needs to allow them to get in here. Once that is done. They will do the rest. And Peets will help us escape!'

The dark haired girl pushed her hair out of her eyes and looked at the small boy.

'Then you need my help,' she said into David's mind, with hope shining in her eyes. 'I have powers as you know. I can heal injury. I can read people's minds. I can move things with my mind. I can see into the future if I allow myself to. I see your parents daily. I can get a message to them. Are you sure that this Peets and Cockroaches and Mantis will really help us? Can they be trusted? We will be very vulnerable if we try to break out and we do not manage to escape. Eldon will punish us severely.'

David considered this. He thought about the little orange Sasquatch. 'Yes' said David in his head. 'I would trust Peets with my life.'

The dark haired girl looked deep into David's eyes. He could feel that she was scanning his very soul.

'OK then' she said into David's head. 'Here's what we are going to do.'

The Elders of Quential

In the light of the early dawn, Chinga, Lamay, Sneets and the scouting party packed up their things. They were starting the long trek today up the mountains of Quential, to speak with the Elders and see if they had seen Peets. And if they hadn't seen him, to find out if anything else could be done to help them find him. If the portal system had worked, Peets should be here. On Quential. Chinga could not give too much thought to the possibility that Peets had ended up going somewhere else due to a malfunctioning portal. If he allowed himself to think about that scenario. His heart would break, because then his boy could be anywhere.

The Elders of Quential lived on the top of a *huge* mountain. The mountain was beautiful and peppered with green, orange and pink trees swaying in the breeze. The mountain was covered with multi-coloured flowers and different varieties of insects, bees and butterflies happily fluttered from flower to flower, busily on their way. If it wasn't for the ache of his heart. Chinga would have felt very at home here. There was a peace and happiness about Quential which almost at times rivalled Delavia. Even the planet itself seemed happy. However this place was not without its tragedies too. Over the past four weeks he had learned that in recent times, their planet was also nearly conquered by evil forces. However this time it was not Valdazar but another faction of evil humans. And *their* leader was called Eldon. It seemed that these humans had a lot to answer for Chinga thought angrily. There seemed to be a lot of them that were really, really bad. However then his thoughts flitted to his friend Isadora, and Orion and Kaia. And he reminded himself that it was not all humans who were bad with a lust for power. Only some. What is it with these humans though? Chinga thought as he slowly trudged up the huge mountain. All they seem to care about is power and 'ruling' over people. Even their own kind? Why can't they all live in peace? The kind of peace that there is here on Quential? Chinga's thoughts focused on the Ancients of his world in Delavia and how they had previously ruled over everyone and kept all the honey to themselves. I suppose there are issues with power even on my own planet he considered. It seems that some people are happy to love and be loved. But others are selfish and just want to dominate. I wonder why this is? It seemed to Chinga to be about Love. Whether you allowed Love to shape your life and your actions, or whether you allowed the Ego to fuel your actions. Whether you spent your life caring for and helping others. Or whether you chose to only look out for yourself.

I know what I choose he thought in his heart. I choose Love.

It would take them three days to scale the huge Mountain of Quential and reach the top.

With Love in his heart, he hoped to god that he would find his little boy up there.

The President

Isadora, Orion and Kaia sat in the Oval Office and in front of the President of the United States. They had landed on the White House Rose Garden Lawn as previously divulged by Kaia. Isadora had tried so hard not to laugh when she saw the look of surprise on the guards shocked face. As a huge Cowboy, a rather tall lady and a normal sized girl, all stepped out of thin air and onto the lawn. As Kaia had cloaked the ship, it could not be seen with the naked eye. So it literally looked like all three of them had appeared out of thin air.

The President smiled at them all behind his huge desk.

'Miss Stone it's great to see you again.' His eyes danced. 'And now' you have more tails of adventure for me? And you must be Orion? The President said looking at the tall Cowboy.

'Yes Sir, That's me! Pleasure to meet you Sir!' Beamed Orion and he stepped forward with an outstretched hand.

The President smiled and stood up to shake the huge Cowboys hand warmly. 'It's a pleasure to meet you too Orion. Thank you for all the help that you gave to Isadora here when you were in Delavia.'

'That's not a problem at all Sir. It is my pleasure to help.' The large Cowboy tipped his hat and sat back down.

The President looked at Kaia. 'And you must be Kaia of Agartha? Wow are all the Agarthans as beautiful as you?' The President smiled as he reached to shake Kaia's hand too.

Kaia smiled. 'You are too kind Mr President' she laughed as she shook the President's hand.

'Right then Isadora,' said the President in his Alpha male tone. 'What news do you have for me today?'

'Well Sir, Isadora began. It is to do with digging.'

'Digging? Said the President in surprise. He sat back in his chair and folded his arms.

'Yes Sir. Apparently us surface humans have been digging down into the Inner Earth lands using our boring tools and this has disturbed the Raptors who live in the top layer of Inner Earth. This has caused the Raptors to move down further inside Inner Earth in order to escape the boring tools that we have been using. As the Raptors have lost territory and hunting grounds, they have now started challenging the Families of Inner Earth for their territory. Up to this point Parmeethius told me that that founding Families of Inner Earth have been able to exist under there in relative peace and each faction has stayed in their own territory of space. However since we have started digging down from the surface it is causing the Inner Earth Families a lot of problems as the Raptors are moving down closer to where they are and have started hanging around their territories. Prior to this the Raptors stayed higher up within the Inner Earth and they had plenty to hunt so there were no problems. Parmeethius told me that there are huge rats under the Earth the size of dogs that the Raptors eat. But our boring tools have been killing a lot of their food sources and so the Raptors have lost both ground and much food. And now they are acting aggressively towards the Inner Earth beings.'

The President had listened to all of this with his mouth set in a hard line and his arms folded under his chest.

He cleared his throat and slowly began to speak.

'Who is Parmeethius Miss Stone?'

'Parmeethius is the head of the Delo Clan Sir, who are the beings I told you about who have purple skin and the features of an elephant.'

'OK.' He said slowly. 'Who are the Raptors?'

Isadora looked at Kaia. 'Kaia could you fill the President in on the Raptors,' she asked shyly. 'I have never even seen them.'

'Of course Isadora. The Raptors Sir, are a dinosaur type race who migrated underground at the time of the great cataclysm that killed off the remaining surface dinosaurs. This race of dinosaur is very clever and enjoys to hunt. It spends much of its time hunting rats and smaller creatures that we have within the Inner Earth. We have tolerated these beings within Inner Earth over the ages as they have kept themselves to themselves in the upper levels of Inner Earth. However as time has moved on their numbers have increased due to breeding and this has coincided with the Humans on the surface boring down into the Earth with your tools. This has resulted in the Raptors doing the only thing they can and digging further down to regain more ground. However they are getting closer and closer to our territories. The Raptors level of Inner Earth is very dark apart from the bioluminescent planets. They do not have access to an inner sun like we do in Agartha. And because of this their eye sight is very poor. They would not be able to hunt on the surface now with the skill that they have in the Inner Earth as their eye sight has adapted to the darkness of Inner Earth and evolved poorly.'

The President listened to Kaia. 'You have an Inner Sun?' He exclaimed. 'A Sun inside the Earth like the one we have in our sky?'

'Yes Sir,' Kaia affirmed. 'We are quite close to the centre of the planet so we are near to the light of the central sun. The Raptors are under the surface but as far away as you can get from the Inner Sun. So their eye sight in light is not great. They have however developed excellent eyesight within darkened, bioluminescent light.'

The President was lost deep in thought. There was what seemed to be a very long pause before he spoke again.

'Kaia, you say that you are a Human of Agartha?'

'Yes that is correct Mr President.'

'Which is inside the Earth?'

'Yes Mr President.'

'So where *is* Agartha? How would I access it from the surface?'

'One could access it from the surface if one was in the Himalayas of Tibet. An entrance to our world can also be accessed through the Great Pyramid of Giza. Through a very long and very large, ancient tunnel. We do however keep entrances to our world guarded at all times Sir. And if anyone from the surface has ever made it to the entrance of our world, who have shall we say, a less than desirous countenance. This in and of itself would ensure that they would never be able to find the entrance itself into our world. In order to enter into Agartha itself. One has to have a very high vibration and a heart of love, otherwise the entrance will not be shown to you. There is only one way that all beings can get into Agartha. And that is through our Technological Portal. However this is highly advanced technology. Much more advanced than anything that you have on the surface and our Technology has never failed us in all the millions of years that Agartha has been our home.'

The President scratched his head trying to process everything that Kaia had been telling him. 'So you guys live under the Earth. And you have everything you need down there? I mean what about food and water? How does that work?'

'We grow our own food under the Earth Sir, using the light from the central sun and the fresh underwater of Gaia. There is twice as much water Sir under the surface of Gaia as there is on your surface. And it is all pure. It is not tainted by pesticides or chemicals from your chem trails. The food we grow under the surface is all vegetables and fruits. Our vegetables and fruits are famed all over the Galaxy and we trade some of our produce off planet at the Galactic markets in order that we might acquire other things which we cannot produce underground.'

'Galactic Markets?' Exclaimed the President quizzically. 'What are those?'

'Much as you have markets in your towns, in your countries on the surface of this world. The wider Galactic community all have a market where they trade their goods which are personal to their planets. All the beings of every planet trade their goods at these markets and this is how people acquire the things that they want. It is all done through trade.' Kaia explained.

The President was starting to realise why some things were kept on a need to know basis for the position of the President. He rubbed his temple and contemplated what had just been revealed to him. Beings that lived inside the Earth had the means to trade their goods, grown inside the Earth, off the planet at a Galactic Market. They could do this as they had spaceships that could take them off planet which were more advanced than what the surface humans had access to. This in and of itself was a President's worst nightmare. How did you protect your country from all of this? Most countries in the Earth alone couldn't stop bickering long enough to find peace. How did you even begin to start with other beings from different planets?

'And this Delo Clan that Isadora has spoken of. The guy with purple skin and elephant face. Who is he?'

'There are lots of different types of beings Sir, who live under the Earth,' Kaia explained. 'There are several old races that all have areas of territory under the Earth. There are several different factions of humans that are tall like us. There's the Delo Clan. There's also a breakaway faction of the Delo Clan called the Dero Clan. And the Delo and The Dero are always in opposition. We have the Amphibian Clans. The Ant People...'

'Ant people?' Shouted the President. 'Next you'll be telling me there's fairies and pixies and little green man running around as well.' He laughed nervously.

'Yes Sir, there are those too but they tend to stay more on the surface of your world instead of coming into the realms of Inner Earth. They have lived on the surface for so long, they prefer it up there now. The gnomes sometimes spend time under the surface. But they tend to do the majority of their work on the surface of the planet. There are also beings that live in your oceans as well Mr President,' Kaia continued. 'Many, many races of different beings that you are unaware of on your surface live in your oceans which are vast. The Mer People of Atlantis who live deep in the ocean also have a base within Inner Earth. Isadora met Pearl today who is the daughter of the leader of their people' Kaia informed.

The President sat and stared at the three friends who were seated in front of his desk. He wanted to laugh all of this off and go back to the life where the things that occupied his mind were fishing and golf. But he knew he couldn't. His brain wanted to laugh off what he had just been told. But his heart knew that he couldn't. They were telling the truth. He had to accept that there was more to the world than he had realised. And as the President, do what he could do to help these people. This was a lot to take in. Especially for someone who was tasked with controlling the country. How could you control what you didn't know about?

'So what is it that you need me to do?' He smiled looking at the unusual trio.

'We need you to stop digging!' the three said in unison.

Bazantire

Human had spent the whole flight to Bazantire memorizing the controls of the ship. He was sure he could fly that thing now. The only thing that concerned him was that his hands would be too small for the ship to recognize. The Valdons had enormous fat, hairy, green hands. He had to find some opportunity to see if the ship's controls would respond to him. If they didn't then he would have to somehow get Isadora and Catherine into the ship without recognizing him. And when they made a few 'hops' back towards Valdar. So probably at Quential. Somehow give the Valdons the slip and find a way to escape from that planet.

It would mean sussing out Quential when they got there and seeing if he could find out who had ships and where the portals were etc. He would have to see if he could make some friends in the short time that he was there, so he had someone to help him when he came back a few weeks later with his wife and daughter.

However for the first stage of the journey they had 'hopped' to Bazantire. Bazantire was still in the same Galaxy as Valdar. Then next hop to Quential would take them to the outskirts of the Milky Way Galaxy. The Galaxy of Earth. Home.

They were to spend three days on Bazantire before the portal system would align towards Quential and they could make their next hop. As the disk shot out of the natural portal on Bazantire. Human walked over to one of the portholes in the ship and looked out at the terrain. This place looked marginally better than the darkness of Valdar. There were slightly less spiky rocks. And a bit more greenery. But essentially it still looked like the same depressing place that they had just come from.

'At least it's not Valdar' thought Human. 'And Valdazar is not here poking me with the death stick. And I am one step closer to returning home and seeing my Wife and Daughter.'

Human was not looking forward to having to spend the next five days in the company of Greb and Than. The two were complete idiots. But it was much better than being with Valdazar. Greb and Than were idiots. But they were predictable idiots. Valdazar was an unpredictable psychopath.

'Why don't you guys go and hunt some food,' said Human to Greb and Than as they landed the ship. 'You must be starving by now. We haven't eaten for a while? I have to contact Master and give him an update on our progress. I will stay with the ship,' Human said.

Greb and Than looked at each other. They didn't particularly fancy listening to Human update the Master. And they were very hungry...

'OK,' said Than. 'Tell the Master we have made it to Bazantire on schedule and in three days will hop to Quential.'

'Yes of course' reassured Human as Greb and Than ambled off the ship and into the terrain to search for something to hunt.

'And now to see if this ship will work for me.' Muttered Human under his breath as he had watched Greb and Than walk into the distance.

Human took a deep breath and put his hands on the huge hand plates. In his mind he 'thought about' the ship rising upwards 10 metres. Time stood still as he waited to see if the ship would respond to him. Slowly the ship began to rise 10 metres in the air and hover there.

'Ha Ha Ha Ha!!!!! YES!!!!' Shouted Human! Wooooooo!'

He thought about the ship returning to the ground and it did so with ease.

Human's heart was racing.

So the ship *did* work for him. He *could* do this. He could really do it.

Quickly he set about contacting Valdazar on the ship's computer. He must make sure that his master was kept happy about everything that was happening and therefore unlikely to do anything rash between now and Human arriving at Earth. Human could not believe it. He could really do this. He could pick up his family and fly his way out of here.

Valdazars face popped up on the screen. 'Well Human?'

It's all going well Sire.' said Human smiling. 'Really well indeed...'

The Plan

The next morning when the bell rang to signal the opening of the door to the exercise yard, David and Aurora slowly made their way towards each other and began walking in unison to the back fence of the exercise pen.

As they reached the back of the yard, both sat down with their backs to the fence, so they could survey the incarcerated human population and any potential threat to their conversation.

'Peets, are you there?' David whispered as loud as he would dare. There was a silence of a second and David heard.

'David! Are you OK? How come you're not hurt? What happened? Why did those boys hit you like that? Who was that dark haired girl? Oh!' Said Peets as he looked up and realised that the dark haired girl was sat next to David. 'You brought the dark haired girl with you to see me! Are you both friends?'

'We are now' whispered David smiling at Aurora. Aurora smiled back.

'Peets Aurora speaks telepathically,' said the little skinny boy. 'Can she fill you in on who she is and what she can do?'

'Yes' said Peets excitedly. 'I'm also telepathic! It's our preferred method of communication on our planet!' Explained the little furry Sasquatch. 'Yes I would love for her to fill me in.'

Aurora sent a series of pictures of her planet into Peets' mind. She showed him the lush trees and forests. She showed him the clean oceans and crisp streams. She showed him the huge majestic mountains and carpets of flowers everywhere. Her people were so happy and free. Laughing and joking, and even flying! Peets wondered how it would feel to be able to fly. How did they do that?

'We do it through our hearts,' laughed Aurora. As they were connected telepathically, Aurora could hear Peets' thoughts. 'We feel the jubilation of flying through our heart space, and in so doing it allows us to soar high up into the sky.'

'Where is this place,' thought Peets? 'And how did you get to be here and incarcerated with David.'

'My planet is called Quential. It is on the edge of the Milky Way Galaxy, which is of course the Galaxy that we are in now. One day the big ships just 'appeared.' They sent little scout ships out which came down and started searching for something on our planet. I now realise that they were looking for me. They realised that Quential was a very powerful planet as we are linked into Source through our hearts and we channel the power of the one true creator. I am the daughter of the founding Elders of Quential. I may look very young but I am in fact very old. I am hundreds of years old. I am the Keeper of the huge Crystal on Quential that channels the power of Source. I have done this all my life since my Mother trained me when I was a young girl. The Crystal responds to me. They took me to weaken the power that my planet has. Also I have powers that they needed to use on this planet. I can see into the future if I project my consciousness there and ask to see an outcome of something. I can heal injury. I can move things with my mind. I can fly on Quential. I don't know if I would be able to do that here,' said the girl sadly. 'Here is not like Quential.'

'Quential sounds incredible,' said Peets. 'We need to get you back there. Has David told you about our plan to break everyone out?'

'Yes' said Aurora. 'I can help with that. I can give you information on all the guards and when they will be asleep, or when they will be walking the perimeter. Eldon is always off planet on a Wednesday. In my visions I see that he goes back to Earth on a Wednesday for a meeting of some sort on that planet. The rest of the time he is either here or off flying around the Galaxy in the big ships looking for more things that they 'need' to do what they are doing here. Eldon is trying to create a deadly weapon that once created, will enable him to blackmail and threaten the rest of the Galaxy to do what he wants to do. He is trying to take over the Galaxy.'

'What is it with these humans and wanting to rule over everyone?' Peets though as his mind returned to his Mother and Sister on Delavia. Had they made it to the caves? Had Father made it back there too?'

Aurora continued. 'There is normally only 1 guard that stays above ground and watches over the sleeping population at night time. The reason being, they know that their technology is sound. And when they lock the individual gates for bed of the individual rooms. They know that there is no way out for the people until morning and the gates are opened once more. So at night time, there is only 1 guard up top. The rest are down below in the underground rooms playing cards, smoking and drinking.'

'So this is good,' thought Peets 'as there will only be 1 guard that we need to deal with in order to get the people out of the compound.'

'Yes said Aurora,' however we have a complication here.'

David looked at Peets very quickly and smiled. Then he turned back round and faced the population again. 'My parents are alive Peets! Whispered David. They are Alive!'

'That is brilliant news my friend! Just brilliant news!' Said the little Sasquatch excitedly. 'How? Where are they?'

'Aurora told me that Eldon took them as he wants them to do some science for him that will give him the scientific figures to create this evil weapon that he's trying to create. My parents were apparently stalling in giving him the information as they knew what Eldon would do with it. However Eldon worked out that this is what they were doing and separated my parents from me. He did this so he could then threaten my parents into giving him the figures, by telling them that he would hurt me if they didn't.'

Peets shook his head. These humans were so very cruel. He just didn't understand why they all couldn't get along. 'So where is Eldon keeping your parents David?'

Aurora answered this question. 'This is the complication I speak about. Eldon has got David's parents locked in one of the underground rooms. I know which room it is. I am taken there daily to work with his parents. Eldon is using me to look into the future to see if their calculations for the weapon will 'work.' This room is at the end of the corridor and in order to free David's parents we will have to walk past the room with the guards. We need to consider how we will do this and not be caught.'

'Not only that, but how will we open the locks on our cells as well Aurora? We can't let others out if we cannot get out ourselves? Questioned David.'

'I am able to move things with my mind David. I will unlock my cell by using my mind. It's a very simple process when you know how. Once I have done this. I will walk out and let you out as well. Then we will need to sneak down the corridor and past the guard. I will ensure that I time this when the guard is sleeping. And then make it to the underground level. Get to your parents without alerting the guards who are playing cards. Free your parents. And then all 4 of us walk past the guards again without being seen. And then to the front entrance. I will then unlock the front entrance with my mind. And then let all of your Cockroach and Bear friends in Peets. Once you guys are in there to deal with the guards and create a diversion, the wider population can then be released and we can guide them up to the Lava Tubes with your help Peets.'

'How will we release the wider population?' Asked David, worrying about how they would pull all of this off.

'There is a red button release for all of the cells on the wall. Where the guard sits. Once Peets and his Cockroach friends have taken care of the guards, we can press the red button release and then everyone will be free.'

'But everyone won't know what to do like we will?' Said David panicking. 'We need to get a message to them that we are going to break out so they are ready!'

'No,' said the beautiful Aurora. 'I have already considered this and looked into the future of what would happen if we let the population know about the breakout before we do it. When Nathan hears he tells his Father who tips off the guards. Then the guards tip off Eldon and he doesn't leave the planet on the Wednesday as he normally would. I know you want to do the right thing David and let everyone know in advance. But if we do that, as there are some bad apples in the mix. It will compromise the mission.'

David frowned. 'So how will we let everyone know that we are breaking out?' The little boy questioned. 'They won't know what to do? They will be scared when they see the Cockroaches and will think they are about to be eaten! And if they see the Bears – they will *really* think that they are about to be eaten! These people have been through enough already. They need peace!'

Aurora was silent for a few moments with her eyes closed.

Finally she spoke into the two comrades heads. 'We cannot allow the mission to be compromised by the few who have bad intent. The ones who have light in their hearts will understand what is happening in the moment. David you and I will quickly run and tell everyone what is happening after we have let in the Cockroaches and the Cockroaches are dealing with the guards. We can hit the release button on the pens and shout to everyone that we are breaking out. I know it will be a lot of confusion. But when something like this happens. People just follow other people like sheep. As long as we shout that we are breaking out and to follow us. People will follow. When they realise that the Cockroaches are not attacking them but just the guards, they will realise what is happening. We have already experienced firsthand how nasty Nathan is. We cannot risk him destroying our only chance of escape. Trust that the Universe has our back and will bring about the highest outcome for us all.'

'OK,' said David reluctantly. 'So how are we going to get to my parents? How will we get past the guards?'

Everyone sat contemplating the mission. There was a lot that could go wrong there for sure. What if the guard heard their cells opening and it woke him up and he shot them? What if they ran into another guard patrolling the corridors and he shot them? What if the Guards playing cards saw them crossing the hall and they shot them? What if the Guards playing cards saw all 4 of them returning back across the hall having freed David's parents? What if they couldn't open the main front door? What if Eldon came back? What if they didn't make it to the Lava tubes in time and they missed the portal home to Delavia?

So many 'what ifs.'

But one thing was certain, they had to try.

The Fairies of Quential

Chinga, Lamay and Sneets had been walking for two days. This mountain was huge! The more you walked, it just seemed to get bigger and bigger! It was the most fascinating mountain that Chinga had ever seen. If his thoughts hadn't constantly been on Peets, he would almost have been having a good time.

The mountain was home to lots of magical creatures that Chinga had never seen before. There were fairies, gnomes, elves, brownies, dwarves. You had to be careful as you were walking along that you didn't step on them! They were all over and they all wanted to come out and say 'hi!' Chinga had introduced himself and his family over a thousand times! These guys were so friendly and they all seemed to want to come out and make their acquaintance. This was great. But it meant that it was taking much longer than Chinga had anticipated to get up this mountain. He had told all of the fairies, gnomes, brownies, elves and dwarves about Peets and asked them to keep an eye out for him. They promised they would and if any of them saw Peets they would spread the word through the network as quick as they could. This had lifted Chinga's spirits no end.

Chinga, Lamay and Sneets were currently laid on the side of the mountain and looking up at the stars. It truly was beautiful. Fairies danced in front of their eyes. Each one lighting up a different colour. In the distance Chinga could hear tiny voices singing. He had a good feeling about this mountain. He hoped and prayed that he would find his Son at the top of it. He really loved this planet. Everyone was so friendly! It's like they all wanted to know his family personally. Every time he had told his story over and over about what had happened to Peets his Son, these little folk had cried. It's like they personally felt his pain. Like they really cared. They had given his family food and told them where the water source was on the mountain. Chinga laughed as he recalled last night. A gnome even gave him a foot massage! All these wonderful beings went out of their way to make Chinga and his family feel at home and happy. If it hadn't have been for the constant ache in Chinga's chest reminding him of the loss of his Son. Chinga would have been blissfully happy. None of their new friends had seen anyone walking up the mountain who looked like them. But that did not mean that Peets wasn't here. There was a portal further up the mountain and Peets could have come through that and walked to the top. In fact Chinga was feeling so happy, he was *sure* that Peets was at the top of the mountain.

Adama

Once more Isadora found herself back in the ship hangar bay in Agartha City. She had really enjoyed seeing the President again. To say he was the President of the United States, he was pretty easy to talk to. He listened to everything that they had told him. And he had promised that he would look into who or why it was that boring tools were being used for digging. And he would make sure that they stopped. He guessed that this was due to fracking or something like that but he wasn't sure and he assured Kaia and Isadora that he would look into it.

Before they had left the White House, the President had given Isadora a very small phone. He was concerned that she was only 15 years old and getting involved in things that could at times be pretty scary. He told her that if she ever needed to reach him, all she had to do was press the red button on the phone. And this was a direct and secure line to his personal number. Isadora had felt very flattered that the President trusted her enough to give her this level of access to him. She had promised that she would carry it with her everywhere. She also thought that he'd given her this phone so she wouldn't contact him on the Smart Pad again. He didn't seem to like that very much!

They had been escorted back down to their ship and within minutes they were back in the hangar bay at Agartha City. Isadora didn't think she would ever get used to how fast these ships could get around.

'So Isadora,' said Kaia smiling. Would you like to say 'Hi' to Adama before we leave or shall I just take you home now?'

'Sure, it would be nice to say Hi to Adama before we left,' Isadora smiled trying to seem casual.

'I think he will be over in the Technology Room. That's where everyone normally hangs out at this time of night.' Kaia explained.

She opened the door and the three filed out and set off for the Technology Room.

'What is the Technology Room Kaia? Asked Isadora. I wonder if it's where they play games? She thought.

'The Technology room is full of seats that are shaped like the long cross section of an egg. We sit in the chairs and we can do a variety of things. We can meditate. We can read anything that has ever been written in the chairs. Both in the Surface Human World and in our world. But instead of playing games like you play in your world. We interact with actual humans through their sleep states. We also view real humans on the surface and watch their lives to see what they have been doing all day.'

'Why would you do that?' Asked Isadora getting grossed out at the thought of being watched all day by the Agarthans. It sounded a bit like the film 'The Truman Show'.

'It's a form of entertainment almost for us Isadora. We like to keep an eye on certain families and make sure that they are OK. We also like to give certain people 'suggestions' which they can then act on which will make your world a better place. So sometimes we will give people suggestions about a new type of technology that we have down here but you don't yet have up there. We are able to interface with your consciousness and pass these new ideas on to your people. Whether the individual decides to act on the idea or not is up to them. But we do try to help the surface humans for the better.'

They kept walking briskly through the rat run caves of Agartha. Isadora was struggling to keep up as Kaia and Orion's legs were so long with them both being so tall.

Finally Kaia stopped in front of an entrance way that opened into a large white coloured room. Inside the room were at least a hundred, large white, half shape eggs. In these eggs sat the Agarthans. It looked like every egg was in use. In some of these eggs there were a handful of children all sat together. In others there were lone individuals. The room seemed very peaceful with very little noise.

'Adama is normally in the back left corner said Kaia. I will stand outside with Orion and we can catch up whilst you say hello to Adama Isadora.'

'Ah, OK,' said Isadora and she gingerly walked into the room. No-one seemed to notice her as she walked into the Technology Room. They were all too in tune with themselves and what it was that they were doing. She kept aiming for the back left corner of the room. And suddenly she saw him. He was as beautiful as ever. Her heart started pounding and she almost started running for the exit through sheer fear. She took a few deep breaths and carried on walking up to where Adama was sat in his egg. She ran a hand over her hair to check it felt OK. She sat in front of Adama at his feet as she wondered how to get his attention. She had never tried to project her consciousness before, it had always been other people that had read her thoughts. She wasn't really sure what to do. But she reasoned that if she could protect her thoughts by placing a bubble of white light around them. Maybe she could project her thoughts to someone else in a bubble too? She began saying 'Hello Adama' in her head and imaging that thought zipping its way across to Adama and dropping into his head.

Suddenly Adama's eyes flicked open and he looked straight at Isadora. He jumped up and picked Isadora clean off the floor and swung her round. Isadora giggled. Someone shouted 'Sshhhhhhhh' from further down the room. Adama whispered 'Sorry' and pulled Isadora into his egg with him. He pulled two silver headsets down from the top of the egg and placed one on each of their heads. The two headsets looked almost like crowns but they were made of a very flimsy, silver material. Isadora was just thinking that she hoped this weird headset hadn't messed up her hair when Adama gestured to Isadora to close her eyes. So she did.

In her mind Isadora could see the most incredible forest. Full of fairies and birds. The leaves themselves sparkled on the trees. It looked like some sort of magical forest. Next she became aware that she was stood in this forest with Adama.

He took her hands and led her towards a beautiful waterfall that was cascading down a bank of rocks to their left. Adama sat down next to the waterfall and Isadora sat down with him.

'So' he said, 'tell me everything! What have you been up to since we got back from Delavia?' The gorgeous Agarthan said and stared deeply into her eyes.

'Erm, me and my Momma went shopping?' Isadora said feeling very embarrassed that she didn't have anything more exciting to tell him. 'And we bought some new slacks! That's pretty much it! What about you?'

'Well since we got back I've stayed pretty close to dad to make sure that he's been healing well. Although there wasn't really much healing to do as the ship pretty much fixed him up. Also I've been back to Delavia a few times to check that the Delavian's are OK. And see if they need any help with anything. They seem to be doing great. The Ancients have lost quite a bit of weight due to not gorging themselves on the honey anymore and they can sort of shuffle around now. The smaller ones are trying to teach them how to walk again. Which is quite funny! I've heard from Orion that Chinga has not found his Son yet?' Adama asked.

'No,' said Isadora sadly. 'The portal on Delavia is not working correctly. Sometimes it does. Sometimes it doesn't. It was aligned at that time to a planet called Quential so I think they are there at the moment looking for Peets. But if he is not there, it's literally going to be like looking for a needle in a haystack as he could be anywhere.'

'I hope they find him,' said Adama gravelly.

'Yes me too,' said Isadora sadly.

'So, I've also been checking in on you from time to time' said Adama shyly.

'How have you done that?' exclaimed Isadora. Horrified at the idea that Adama was able to see her at all.

'When you've been asleep. I've tried to interface with your consciousness so I could appear in your dreams!' the beautiful Agarthan said shyly.

'I have been dreaming about you an awful lot!' Said Isadora embarrassed. 'So when you've been in my dreams, have you actually been there?'

'My consciousness has!' Said Adama. 'But I've been sat here in this egg. I've been trying to reach you most nights. Some nights I can. But others I've not been able to get through. As even in your sleep, you've had that white light shield up.'

'Yes, I have been practicing when I've gone to bed. Like every night!' She laughed. 'I didn't want you to be able to read my thoughts the next time I saw you. And now I find out you've been stalking me in my dreams!' she laughed.

'Do you want me to stop?' Said Adama seriously. 'I won't come into your dreams if you don't want me to.'

'No,' she said hurriedly.' I *want* to see you. I've missed you so much. I've thought about you every day since we came back. But I've tried not to as your Father told me it was not possible for an Agarthan and a Surface Human to be together.' She looked down feeling that maybe she had said too much. She didn't want this time with Adama to ever end.

Adama frowned and looked down. 'My Father has set ideas about the way things have been and the way they have preserved their way of life down here for so long. But things are changing Isadora. I see a world where Agarthans and Surface Humans can live together. It won't be too much longer. So much is changing.' He paused and touched her face. 'I don't think it will be too much longer before we will be able to come to the surface and introduce ourselves. I mean you've been to see your President today haven't you with Kaia? And the President was fine with meeting her and Orion wasn't he?'

'Yes' nodded Isadora. 'The President thought she was very beautiful and he said so to her face.'

'I think *you're* very beautiful' said Adama and he leaned in closer to Isadora's face.

'Thankyou' she breathed and she closed the gap between them.

This time she kissed him.

Under a carpet of stars and next to the sound of a waterfall.

She knew they weren't 'really' kissing as in real life their bodies were sat side by side, next to each other in the strange white shaped egg.

But in whatever reality this was. This dream world where they could interact and talk to each other. This kiss felt as real as the last one had. The first time Adama had ever kissed Isadora, after the feast. Only this one was better as now she really had feelings for Adama. She really hoped he was right about the future of his people and it being a possibility that Agarthans and Surface Humans could mix. She had to believe this was a possibility.

They two pulled apart and stared into each other's eyes.

'I wish you could stay' whispered Adama staring sadly into Isadora's eyes.

'Me too,' she agreed shyly. 'But I have a feeling that we are going to be seeing a lot of each other in the future. There's so much going on. And it seems somehow, because of my friendship with Chinga, I've become the link to the President in our world for your people. Like I have no idea how this has happened,' she laughed.

Adama smiled. 'I'm so glad that you are the ambassador of the surface humans,' he teased. 'And that I have had the opportunity to meet you. Imagine if it was someone else that Chinga had met in the forest and made friends with! But it wasn't, it was you. And now here we are.'

Isadora smiled shyly. 'So like in Agartha, is there someone here that your Father wants you to marry when you are ready?' She said nervously, afraid of the answer.

Adama frowned and looked away at the waterfall. What seemed like an age passed before he spoke again. 'Yes, there is a girl that my Father has picked out for me to partner with should I want to do that. And have children. But I do not feel that I want to do that with her. I have not been interested in anyone. Until I met you. I have always been so focused on learning all there is to learn and also training physically so I can defend Agartha should it ever need defending. My thoughts have never been on Love. Until I met you.'

Isadora's heart stopped beating. He had said the 'L' word.
Surface boys had a lot to learn from these Agarthans she thought happily!

Quential

Human's time on Bazantire was over and they were just waiting for the portal system to open that was aligned to Quential. It had been the longest three days of Human's life. Focused mainly on listening to Greg and Than bickering and moaning about being hungry. All these great lumps did is eat; eat and moan and sleep. Yet the time had passed and here they were waiting for the portal to open to Quential. As soon as the portal opened up like a shimmering bubble, Greb directed the little ship into it. And POP. Just like that, they were now on Quential.

Quential looks much better than the last place thought Human excitedly.

The Vegetation looked incredible! Beautiful trees and flowers. The portal system had brought them out about 10 metres from the surface and halfway up what looked to be a *huge* mountain.

'Let's get parked up and go find some food,' said Greb. 'I'm starving.' Human rolled his eyes. All this beauty in front of their eyes and still all the Valdons could think about was their stomachs.

Greb slowly lowered down the little ship onto the side of the mountain and under a canopy of trees. It was very fortunate that they had parked directly in front of a small stream that ran down the mountain, as Human had noted that they were nearly out of water. There wasn't much to be found on Bazantire.

The two Valdons ambled out of the ship and set off looking for some food to hunt. Human slowly stretched his aching muscles and walked down off the little ship. Finally for the first time in a very long time, he was alone. Alone and at leisure to do what he wanted to do. The Valdons would be gone for a while. They were not the most nimble of creatures so it always took them an age to catch anything. This would give him time to have a wash in the stream. He had not been able to wash for a very long time. And that stream looked incredible.

He undid his cloak which fastened under his chin and dropped that to the floor. That was so liberating. He had not been able to take that cloak off in the day since the day Valdazar had made him begin wearing it. Next he took off his shoes and socks. He squinted down at his toes. He had not looked at his own toes in a very long time. They were still attached to his feet he mused. He bent down to look at the water and splashed some onto his face. He placed his toes into the stream. One then the other. The water was so cold and refreshing. It almost made Human want to cry. He had been so numb since he had been broken by Valdazar. But today he felt alive. He felt hope in his chest as he was on his way home. As he looked into the stream the water was crystal clear. He saw the reflection in the water of a fairy flying next to his head. Wow, he thought. This planet was really special. Fairies too? As he brought his face up and rubbed it clean in order to get a better look. He had never seen a fairy before in real life. He stared at the fairy and the fairy smiled and waved. Human smiled and waved back. Suddenly he heard a sharp intake of breath from across the stream and someone gasp 'Oh No! What's *he* doing here?'

He spun round quickly to see where the voice had come from. Was that directed at him? Surely no-one here knew who he was? He was no-one. All Human managed to catch out of the corner of his eye was a little ball of orange brown fur retreating into the distance. They can't have meant me he thought. They probably can't even see me. I am used to blending into the background. Human closed his eyes and concentrated on the feeling of the cool water rushing over his toes.

Sneets

Sneets had woken up early that morning and excitedly ran to the stream to fill up their water bottles for the journey ahead. They were hoping if they did a really big push today, they would make it the rest of the way up the Mountain before Sunset. If it proved too difficult, they would of course take two days for the journey. But they had woken up optimistic that they could complete the ascent in a day. Thoughts of Peets pushed them to exert themselves.

As Sneets had ran excitedly to the stream the sight of Human had stopped her in her tracks. She was horrified. Fear ran up her spine as she processed what she was seeing. She could not believe her eyes. What was he doing on Quential? And was Valdazar with him and those scary Valdons? Why were they here? Were they looking for her brother too? What did they want with him? He was only a young Sasquatch. Had they re-taken Delavia whilst they had been away looking for her brother and now they were trying to find them too? She ran as fast as her little legs would carry her and back to her Mother and Father.

'Mother, Father!' She shouted as she saw their fur through the trees. 'We have to leave now!' She screamed.

'What is it my love!' said Lamay, 'what has happened?'

'Mother I've just seen that man, the man who was with Valdazar who translated what the Ancients said? He was here in the forest?'

'Here in the forest,' said Lamay in a panic. 'But I thought they left and went back to Valdar? What are they doing here?'

Chinga who had been listening to this conversation walked up to his daughter and tried to calm her down.

'Sneets my love, we blew up Valdazar's ship remember? Well General Myers did, when he started shooting at everything in sight! I was so angry as I thought I had lost you all! He killed Valdazar and the Valdons that day when he blew up their ship? They were on it. It must be someone else you just saw who looked like that man my love.'

Lamay turned to look at Chinga with horror on her face. 'No my love, Valdazar and the Valdons weren't on that ship that blew up. They left on another ship the night before you came. A group of merchants came to Delavia and Valdazar traded some of our honey for a ship of theirs. And he left in *that* ship with the majority of his army. He only left 20 behind to guard us. Valdazar and the Valdons aren't dead. They are still very much alive!'

'And I would recognize one of *them* anywhere' said Sneets in disgust.

Chinga looked at his wife and daughter in disbelief. Valdazar and the Valdons were still alive? How could this be? He sat down slowly and considered this. If Valdazar was still alive, then he would be really, really angry when he found out that Delavia had been taken back. Valdazar was not to be messed with. There would be retaliation for what they had done. Is that why he was here now? Was he here to find him and his family for the part he had played? He had after all turned up on one of the big ships that had taken Delavia back. And what about his friend Isadora and Kaia. They would be in danger too if Valdazar was still alive.

Chinga felt sick.

He had to warn Isadora and Kaia that Valdazar was still alive.

'Quick,' said Chinga in a low serious voice. 'We have no time to lose. We must get to the top of this mountain today. If Valdazar and the Valdons are here then it is no longer safe for us. We need to get up this Mountain and find out if Peets is up there. If not we need to get off this planet as quick as possible and inform my friends on Earth that Valdazar is in fact still alive. There has been a massive misunderstanding here. We thought Valdazar and his army had been blown up when General Myers attacked their ship. And now you tell me that Valdazar had left a day earlier on *another* ship? Valdazar will know by now that Delavia has been taken back. 4 weeks have passed since we have left. He will be angry. Very angry. And Valdazar is not to be messed with. If he is here then he is looking for us. And he will be looking for revenge. We must get to the top of the mountain as quickly as we can. There is no time to lose,' said Chinga gravely.

'I cannot believe you have not mentioned this before now my loves.'

Lamay and Sneets looked at each other for reassurance. 'I am sorry my Love,' said Lamay, 'we did not *realise* that you didn't know. *Of course you didn't know.* It happened before you arrived. But, Yes Valdazar and the majority of his army left with him on that new ship before you arrived.'

Chinga shook his head. He could not believe this new development.

'And now he is here,' cried Sneets. Her face in her hands. 'What if he captures us again? This place is so lovely. I couldn't bare it if he caged all of these wonderful creatures. The fairies would not survive!'

'We need to get up this Mountain my love and warn the Elders.' Said Chinga in haste and he began the ascent up the mountain.

And he had to find his Son, now!

The Breakout

David and Aurora sat opposite each other again in the canteen at breakfast. Both pushed their food around their plates and didn't speak. To the rest of the population they looked like two kids ignoring each other and playing with their food.

Little did everyone know that telepathically David and Aurora were devising their plan of escape.

It had to be done on a Wednesday as Eldon would not be there. He would be on Earth. Wednesday was tomorrow night. Could they do it tomorrow or should they wait another week? Aurora would wait till the guard was asleep and let herself out of her cell. She would then let David out of his cell. The two would then run down to the lower level and free his parents.

They were currently trying to establish how they would get past the room of guards without alerting them.

'I am able to project images with my mind.' Said Aurora her mind working overtime. 'So maybe I could project an image of a bare wall in front of the guard's entrance way as we slip across behind it?'

David didn't really understand what she meant but he tried his best. 'You mean project a 'picture' of the wall in place across the doorway. But really that's just a fake image and we can pass behind it?'

'Yes that's right,' said Aurora. 'Then I'll have to let that image drop so they see the real wall. Go and open your parents' door with my mind. Then run back and project the image of the wall again so we can then all pass behind it once more and up to the front entrance. Then once we get to the front entrance. I will open that with my mind and we will let the Bears and Cockroaches in. They can then deal with the guard upstairs and those on the lower levels. And we can press the red button release on the wall and release all of the cells. We can quickly shout to everyone that we are breaking out and to follow us.

Then we go. The Cockroaches will do the rest at the facility. Then we can start the run up to the Lava Tubes. Do we know how to get to the Lava tubes?' Aurora asked David.

'I'm guessing Peets knows said David as that's where the portal is for him to get home.'

'And do we know where the portal is aligned to the night that we are breaking out? Where are we going to end up?' Aurora checked.

'Ah I don't know,' said David. 'But anywhere is better than here right? We just need to get away from these guys and then when we are on another planet, we can then work out how to get back to our home planets. I don't know if my parents would want to go back to Earth now,' said David quietly. 'It's been 35 years since Eldon brought them here. They were 20 years old when he brought them here. Two of the top scientific minds in their college year. Mum was 47 when she had me,' David explained. 'I wasn't meant to happen. Mum and Dad always said they would never bring a child into this place. But when they had me, Mum said that I was the best mistake they had ever made. That I had given them hope. Will you see them today?' Asked David sadly. He missed his parents so much.

'Yes,' said Aurora. 'I am taken to them daily to check that the figures they are giving Eldon are correct by looking into the future.'

'How does that work?' Asked David quizzically.

'I look at the information and I focus on Eldon and your parents and I view the possible futures that can come from the information that I have been given.' Aurora explained.

David shook his head. 'That seems really complicated to me. How will you let my parents know that we are going to be breaking out on Wednesday? Is Eldon there the whole time you are there with them?'

'Yes,' confirmed Aurora sadly. 'I can try and see if I can connect with them telepathically to pass on the message. But if I cannot connect to them then it will just have to be a surprise for them, like it will be a surprise for everyone else.'

Both of them sat lost deep in thought.

'We'll have to make sure we don't wake up the guard' David said worrying. 'And what happens if Eldon comes back in his ship whilst we are making our escape.'

'We run' said Aurora with a look of determination on her face.

The Portal Map

Peets had met with David and Aurora at morning break. They had spent a good amount of time at breakfast devising their plan and Peets thought it was great. He was on his way back to the caves now to tell Koro about their plans and see if Koro had any changes that needed making. If there were any changes to be made, Peets could let David and Aurora know tomorrow morning at morning exercise break. Then they would be there ready and waiting for them when they broke out tomorrow night. Peets had butterflies in his tummy. He was really going home.

Peets ran into Koro's familiar cave.

'What news little one?' Said the kind, shaggy Bear.

'David and Aurora want to break out tomorrow night as Eldon always goes to Earth on a Wednesday and he will not be here.'

The large Bear frowned. 'Shouldn't we wait another week in order to finalise our plans?'

'I think we need to see the portal map Koro,' said Peets in earnest. 'It's no good everyone breaking out tomorrow night if we can't go anywhere? What will we do then? Now we have a solid plan in place. Can we ask Sylas if we can look at his portal map and see when it goes back to Delavia?'

'Yes,' sighed the huge Bear. 'I feel that you are right. It is time that we take our information to The Cockroaches and ask them for a glance at the portal map so we can help you plan your escape. Time to visit Sylas once more.'

Peets was not looking forward to that. But he was excited. As the time for waiting was over. Finally he would be going home. Finally he would see his Mother and Sister and hopefully his Father again. He would miss Koro very much. He had grown very fond of the huge kind Bear whilst he had stayed with him on Mars. Koro had shown him so much kindness. He did not know what he would have done without him. Without Koro he likely would not still be alive.

'Thankyou Koro,' said the little orange Sasquatch, 'for all you have done for me whilst I have been here. If it wasn't for you, I probably would not still be alive. Thankyou from the bottom of my heart for helping me and allowing me to stay with you whilst I have been here. One day I promise I will repay your kindness to me.'

The large Bear smiled at the little furry boy. 'There is no need to thank me little one. I did what anyone with a heart would do.'

Peets smiled at Koro. He was going home.

The Journey Back Home

Isadora and Adama's reunion was rudely interrupted by the sound of Kaia's voice.

'Isadora, it's time to go. Can you hear me? It's time to go.'

Isadora opened her eyes and remembered that she was sat in the egg with Adama. They still had their little silver headsets on. And they were holding hands. Nothing looked too suspicious to the outside world.

Then she noticed that Kaia had a silver headset from that egg on her head too. She coloured up. Had Kaia seen them kissing?

'It's time to go Isadora,' said Kaia. 'We need to get you back home before your Mother realises that you aren't there. We've checked on her whilst you've been here. She's asleep. I will give you a few minutes to say your goodbyes. I'll wait by the door.'

Isadora watched Kaia stride off and then turned to Adama.

They looked into each other's eyes. Happy at what they had just shared. But both sad as they had no idea when they would have the opportunity to see each other again.

'I will be in your dreams every night when you are asleep Isadora.' Said Adama quietly. 'Look out for me?'

He leaned over and kissed her gently on the lips. For real this time. Isadora felt light headed. His smell was intoxicating.

'Yes, I will look out for you every night.' She squeezed his hand. 'Until next time.' She leaned and kissed him once more on the lips and then got up and strode out of the Technology room. She really did not want to leave him. All she wanted to do was run back and jump into his arms. She felt tears well up in her eyes and sadness in her chest.

As she got to the door Kaia was waiting there as promised.

'Orion will fly you back Isadora as he is going on somewhere else.'

The tall, beautiful Cowboy extended his arm and invited Isadora to link arms with him.

'I'll see you soon Kaia?' Asked Isadora with so many questions in her voice? What she really meant was 'Will I get to see Adama again soon?'

'Yes Isadora.' Said Kaia, her eyes dancing. 'We will see you soon. We will need to give you an update on the digging situation in a week or two. Once we see if the President is able to stop them from digging. You will be back down here again with us before you know it. When do you start back at school again?' Asked the beautiful Agarthan.

'Don't mention school' Isadora groaned through gritted teeth. 'I go back in around two weeks.'

'Well we will make sure that we see you again before you go back and give you an update.'

'OK,' said Isadora. 'I guess I'd better get back home and check on my Momma.'

'It will be my pleasure to escort you home Ma'am,' drawled Orion. 'Give us time to have a proper catch up,' the Cowboy winked.

Quential

Human really liked this place. Pity they were only here for a day and not three like on Bazantire. Maybe he could come back here after he had rescued Isadora and Catherine? There was all sorts of life here. Creatures that he had heard about in the nursery rhymes of Earth, but never seen with his own eyes. It truly was magical.

Whilst the Valdons had been gone searching for food, he had chatted to the fairies, some elves and even some gnomes! They could all talk! And they were all really friendly. He was doing his best to make friends here in case he needed to stop off back here with Catherine and Isadora. It would be good to have some friends to rely on. The Valdons had been gone for hours. Most of the day in fact, and he was really starting to enjoy himself.

He was currently having a rather pleasant conversation with a pixie when Greb and Than walked back through the trees holding three dwarves upside down and by their legs.

The pixie looked up horrified at the sight of the gargantuan Valdons holding three of his friends by the legs and waving them around as if they were little rag dolls. The pixie screamed and ran off to fetch re-enforcements.

'These was all we could find,' slurred Than. 'There's no cows here. But we found these little men. They'll have to do until we get to Earth. I don't think they have cows on the Moon do they? How long are we ere for?' Asked Than.

Human sighed at the sight of the huge Valdons. Of course they were eating the magical creatures. Of course they were. The only thing they ever thought about was food. And doing anything their evil Master said.

'Only a day here,' said Human. Unfortunately he thought. 'We leave for the Moon in the early hours of the morning. I'm sure I saw some cows out of the window when we came through the portal, Human lied. Why don't you let the little guys go? There won't be much meat on them. In fact, I was just talking to that little pixie guy, and he said that the Dwarves give you terrible heartburn. Absolutely terrible. He said that there were cows at the bottom of the mountain. You could take the ship down and back in a couple of minutes? Much better to do that than have heartburn.'

Greb and Than considered what Human was saying. They hated heartburn. And they loved cows. And these little guys didn't look like they would fill them up.

'Alright,' said Greb. Dropping the two dwarves that he held on the floor. The two little men rubbed their heads and their bottoms and quickly ran off into the trees. Than followed suit and dropped his dwarf. The little man whispered 'thankyou' to Human as he ran off into the undergrowth.

'There better be cows darn there,' shouted Greb. 'Otherwise you're goin in the pot!' he shouted at Human as he stalked off to the ship.

The Elders

Chinga, Lamay and Sneets had ploughed up the rest of the way of the mountain in record time. Fear had pressed them on. Was Valdazar looking for them? Why was he here? Had he re-taken Delavia? Were their people safe? Was Peets with the Elders at the top of this mountain? They had not stopped to rest or eat all day. It was just before sunset when they finally reached the top of the mountain.

Their chests heaving, they scanned the horizon. No sign of Peets at the top of this mountain on first inspection. Another part of Chinga's heart broke.

However, on the top of the Mountain stood the most spectacular palace that Chinga had ever seen. Well really it was the *only* palace that Chinga had ever seen. The reason it was so spectacular was because it was made of light. It twinkled an iridescent pink and purple colour. It looked like the colour you get inside of bubbles. The inside of shells. Beautiful rainbow iridescence.

The sight of this magnificent palace stopped them in their tracks for a bit. And they drank the beauty in. Finally Chinga said, 'Come, let us speak with the Elders and see if they have news for us of our Son.'

Chinga, Lamay and Sneets gingerly approached the large shimmering palace and walked inside. There were no doors. No guards. Nothing from stopping them making their way inside the beautiful home.

As they walked into the palace of light, they became aware of a gigantic Crystal in the middle of the palace. It was beautiful. It was at first glance white. But upon further inspection Chinga noticed as he gazed into the Crystal that he could see so many colours swirling around inside. He also saw areas that looked like space and galaxies held within the heart of the Crystal. What was that thing?

His musings were interrupted by the entrance of a very beautiful woman. She had hair the colour of Saffron and it cascaded down her back in long soft curls. She had the most beautiful face and her body was kept modest by straps of gold material that were strategically placed. A beautiful white light glistened all around her body. She was breath-taking.

'Have you brought us news of our daughter?' The beautiful woman asked?

'Ah no,' said Chinga suddenly feeling embarrassed that they had walked into this woman's home. 'We come to ask you if you have news of our Son?'

The beautiful woman frowned and looked down at her feet in sadness and back up at the tall orange, furry man. 'Who is your Son?' She said with compassion in her face.

'My name is Chinga and I come from a planet called Delavia. A couple of months ago we were attacked by a human called Valdazar who is a psychopath and has systematically taken over every planet in his own Galaxy. He moved into our Galaxy and took our planet Delavia. Delavia is famed for its honey and that's why Valdazar conquered our planet. I was on Earth at the time but through my friend Isadora I managed to put together a party of people who travelled to Delavia and took the planet back. We thought we had destroyed Valdazar and his army when we blew up his ship that was parked in the sky there. But I just found out today that Valdazar had left earlier on before we got there in another ship and he is still at large. My daughter today also saw Valdazar's telepath on your mountain. Valdazar never travels anywhere without his telepath. So if he is here, then Valdazar is also here. I would strongly advise you to gather up your people and get everyone to safety before the rest of his army makes it here.'

Chinga continued, 'Also my Son left my home planet of Delavia looking for me when I was on Earth. However he didn't understand that at the time the portal system was aligned to your planet of Quential and not Earth. We believe our Son came here around 4 weeks ago and we have been searching your planet to try and find him. We have searched in as many places as we can. But probably not all places. We have travelled up this mountain to ask you Elders if you have seen our Son. And if you have not seen him. Is there anything you can do to help us at least find out if he is indeed on your planet?

'I have not seen your Son,' said the beautiful woman with the Saffron hair. 'I have not seen anyone since the Humans came and took my daughter away.' Tears glistened in the beautiful woman's eyes.

Chinga looked down at his feet trying really hard not to cry.
'Who took your daughter?' Asked Chinga. 'I'm so sorry. I know how it feels to be separated from your child. And it hurts like hell.'

'Yes,' said the flame haired woman who walked closer to the Sasquatch family. 'They came on big ships many months ago. They wanted to know where our special powers come from. How we are able to fly and move things with our minds. But we couldn't show them as they have different hearts to us. Different consciousness. They could not harness the power of Source as we do as they are not of a high enough vibration.'

'Vibration?' asked Chinga. 'What do you mean?'

'Everything is vibration. To be able to fly and move mass with your mind you have to be of a high vibration. You have to be in harmony with the Universe. You have to be in the vibration of Love. These humans are in the vibration of service to self and only seek power over others. Due to this they will never be able to fly. Not unless they use technology to do so. They were angry with us and fearful that we had more powers than them. They took my daughter. My daughter harnesses the power of Source here through the great Crystal, she said pointing to the huge white Crystal in the centre of the palace. There is much I can do with the Crystal, but my daughter is the

Crystals preferred choice. My daughter works with the Crystal to channel Love and Light into our world here. They said if we did not retaliate they would bring her back to us in a few months. They needed to use her for some task that they have.'

'These humans,' asked Chinga. 'Was their leader someone called 'Valdazar?'

'No,' said the beautiful woman sadly. 'The leaders' name was 'Eldon.'

'Did they have huge, ugly green creatures with them that were really stupid? But very strong?' Chinga asked.

'No, they all looked to be of Human form. But they had many ships. And there were too many of them for us to fight. We are not accustomed to fighting on Quential. We are a planet of Love and Light. We look after all of our people. All of our kingdoms here on Quential. We do not really understand how to fight. How to be that cruel. We only know Love here. They told me that they would bring my daughter back in a few weeks. But it has been many months now and I fear that they will not bring her back. And I do not know where they have taken her. I do not know where they have gone.' The beautiful lady with the orange hair began crying. Sobbing tears of grief and sadness. Lamay walked over to her and wrapped her arms around her and began to cry too. They supported each other in their grief. Two mothers who have both suffered the loss of their children. Never knowing if they would see them again.

Chinga struggled himself to push his tears down. There had to be something that they could do. He could go back to Earth and speak with Orion and Kaia and see if they knew anything about this Eldon character. He could see if he could help this woman.

'I'm sorry,' said Chinga. 'In my haste to ask about my Son, I never introduced my family. This is my wife Lamay,' he said pointing to Lamay. The two ladies pulled apart from each other and looked at each other shyly. 'And this is my daughter Sneets,' said Chinga. 'My

Son Peets looks almost identical to Sneets,' Chinga said with sadness in his heart. 'I have friends on Earth who I could ask to help us find your daughter. We could look for my Son and your daughter together? I'm sure my friends on Earth will have heard of this Eldon guy and will be able to point us in the right direction.'

'Thank you for your help my friend,' said the beautiful lady wrapped in gold. 'My name is Aria and I am one of the Elders of Quential. My partner and Aurora's Father is Leonadis. Leonadis has taken our only ship and is out looking for Eldon at the moment. I have stayed here in case they bring Aurora back. What else can I do?'

The Cockroaches

Once again Peets and Koro stood in front of Sylas the king of the Cockroaches.

Koro had just filled Sylas in with the plans of David and Aurora and Sylas was smiling an evil smile.

'So tomorrow night we break in and take our land back Koro?' The large Cockroach said happily. 'And I suppose you want to see my portal map now in order that you might plan your escape?' The smelly insect asked Peets.

'Depending on what the portal map says Sylas. The breakout will either be tomorrow night or a week tomorrow.' Said the large Bear. 'Whichever week will get our friend the nearest to his home planet of Delavia.'

'I see,' nodded the large Cockroach. 'Bring the portal map,' Sylas ordered his Cockroach guard.

The giant Cockroach scuttled off and seconds later was back with a very large and very old piece paper. Actually as Peets focused on the portal map, it became clear to him that this was no ordinary piece of paper. Peets did not want to think about what that portal map was made out of. The Cockroach guard passed the map to Sylas. Sylas began to study it.

'So the breakout is either tomorrow night or Wednesday next week is that correct?' The disgusting Cockroach spat.

'Yes that is correct,' said the Bear quietly.

'It has taken me years to learn how to study this map' said Sylas with an evil smile. 'I traded it for a number of my Cockroach people who were needed to work on Unatron. We will always have plenty of Cockroaches here, but it's not every day that you come across a portal map,' the large bug laughed.

Peets did not like Sylas at all. He made his flesh crawl. He did not trust him. Not at all. Anyone who would trade some of his own people for a map was not to be trusted. But what choice did he have?

'Looking at this map your hairy orange friend here has several choices,' said the large smelly Cockroach. 'If you break out tomorrow night. The portal in the Lava tubes is aligned to Bazantire from 8pm – 11pm and Quential from 11pm to 3am. If you break out next week the portal is aligned to Sirius A from 8pm – 11pm and Sirius B from 11pm – 3am. What will it be Koro? Am I galvanizing my troops this week or next week?'

Koro looked at his furry orange friend and awaited a decision.

Peets swallowed down a sense of sadness. He wouldn't be going home tomorrow. And neither would David. But they could get their friend Aurora home and back to Quential. When they were safe there, he could always make it back to Delavia then. What difference would a few more days make? He was just grateful that he had at least heard of one of the planets before.

'Tomorrow night,' said the little Sasquatch. 'I will ask David and Aurora to open the main doors at 12 midnight. We need all of the Cockroaches and Bears that you have to storm the facility and deal with the guards. And also help the general population get up to the portal in the Lava tubes. Koro and I will help David and Aurora get up to the Lava tubes as soon as the main door is opened. Then you can direct the rest of the population to follow us,' said the little Sasquatch. 'They will be able to see where we are going.'

'OK,' smiled the evil Cockroach, 'I will inform my troops. They will be there for 12 midnight. I will also speak with the Mantis of the tubes tonight and let them know you will be coming tomorrow night to use their portal. They have already agreed your passing through the portal in exchange for the riddance of the human stronghold,' Sylas confirmed.

'I will speak with the rest of the Bears,' said Koro 'and we will help the population get up to the Lava tubes. Perhaps you would prefer to deal with the guards my friend?' Said Koro to Sylas.

'Oh Yes Koro,' laughed the disgusting bug. 'It will be my absolute pleasure.'

Orion

Orion and Isadora walked slowly back to the hangar bay in Agartha City. It seemed that Orion wasn't in a hurry to get home either. I wonder where he lives she thought.

'Orion, where do you live?' Asked Isadora inquisitively.

'I don't really *live* anywhere Ma'am,' drawled the handsome Cowboy. 'I don't need to sleep much see. So because I don't need to sleep much. I don't really live anywhere. I'm always working Miss Isadora. There's lots that's goes on, on this planet of yours and it's my job as well as others like me to keep it safe. As much as we can.'

Isadora considered this. He must go *somewhere*.

'Well, where will you go now?' Continued Isadora. 'If I'm going to go home and go to bed. What will you do now?'

'I do not have any other directions for the rest of today Ma'am, so after taking you home. I will most probably fly into Area 51 and catch up with the guys there. See what's been happening down there and if they need my help with anything. If everything is all good there then I might go and visit friends.'

'In the middle of the night?' Exclaimed Isadora. 'Who would be up in the middle of the night?'

'Don't forget Miss Isadora, not everyone on this planet is human. So not everyone needs to sleep. There's plenty of folk that I know that will be up all night. My friend Sammy is an Antarean from Antares. You wouldn't know it to look at him as he uses a human form here. He breeds horses. I like to go there sometimes at night when it's real quiet and ride the horses. I like looking after them.' The huge Cowboy said as he helped Isadora climb up into the spaceship.

'So Orion,' asked Isadora, 'how many 'aliens' are there on our planet? Because as you know. No-one has got any clue? Like, we're taught in school that there is only us humans in the entire Universe and we're top of the food chain.'

'Miss Isadora,' said Orion in a joking tone. 'Consider how vast the Universe is. Do you think it likely that the only planet in the entire Universe that is comprised of an infinite amount of stars and planets, to have life on, is Earth? How likely does that seem?'

'Not very likely,' she said quietly.

'Not very likely *at all*, I would say! Also where do all your legends of Fairies and Mermaids and Dragons and Unicorns come from? If they are not real? Also how can you account for all of the UFO sightings that people see? But the biggest question for you right now is. How do you account for an 8 foot tall Cowboy from Alpha Centauri flying you home in this spaceship. If I am in fact, not real?'

Isadora frowned. 'But I just don't get it *Orion!*' She said. 'Why don't we know about any of this stuff? Why have they kept it from us? Where have the Fairies and Mermaids and Unicorns and Dragons gone? None of this makes any sense to me,' she sighed.

'This is a quite complex topic Ma'am and I don't want to say too much and scare you now. But I also realise that now you are being subjected to this world. You need to know what you are dealing with. So where do I begin?' Drawled the beautiful Cowboy. 'OK, this Universe is based on Duality. Duality is Dark and Light. And essentially this entire Universe is a dance between dark and light. At one time, surface humans on Earth could see the Fairies and Mermaids and Unicorns etc. because they were at the same vibration as them in their consciousness. Everything is vibration and frequency, Isadora. Whatever matches your vibrational frequency in the Universe you will be able to see. However back when Humans were experimenting with things they should not have been. In the times of Atlantis. When the Galactic Council allowed Atlantis to fall. Human consciousness also fell with it. The Atlanteans had been undertaking terrible experiments on beings there. They had been fashioning together horrifying creatures through using their consciousness to create these beings. There was no thought given to the quality of these creatures lives. They just became a form of entertainment for the Atlanteans. And sometimes they made these creatures fight with each other. And fight to the death. They made significant advancements in Science and Technology but they left behind spirituality and whether they *should* be doing the things that they were doing. When they started harnessing the power of the great Crystals within the Earth, it was decided that the Atlantean Civilisation with their cruel ways had gone far enough. And the City was allowed to fall into the sea through a great cataclysm.

Atlantis was both above ground and under water and the underwater part of Atlantis remains to this day. However most of you Earth Humans are unable to see it as it is in a much higher vibrational frequency than what you resonate at currently.

Since the fall of Atlantis, as your frequency fell so low. This left an opening for other beings who harvest energy to come in and control your population. These beings live on Earth too but are on a different dimension that is negatively polarised. They have kept you in the dark as to the fact that you are not alone in the Universe as this has suited their agenda. They essentially feed off the energy of human misery. This is why there are so many wars on your planet. It is all orchestrated by these beings.'

Isadora shook her head. This was all a little too much for her for this time of night. She was so tired. And she just could not get her head around what Orion was saying to her. Other beings in different dimensions that fed off the human's energy? That seemed really far-fetched.

'Orion, can we talk about this in more detail some other time when I'm more awake? It's kind of blowing my mind.'

'Sure Ma'am,' smiled Orion. 'It's a lot to take in. We'll pick it up some other time.'

The two flew on in silence.

'A couple of minutes and I'll have you back home Ma'am,' said the handsome Cowboy.

More silence.

Then suddenly Isadora thought of something that she had been meaning to ask Orion.

'Orion, do you remember when we met Ebanon that time? He let us use his portal out of his underground base and that's how we got to Agartha?'

'Yes,' said Orion.

'Well I was wondering. It seemed to me like you and Ebanon had some past history or something. Like Ebanon was indebted to you for something?'

'You are very observant Miss Isadora, truly you are.' Laughed the Cowboy. Me and Ebanon go back a ways.'

'So what's the deal?' she pressed.

Orion went quiet, lost in thought. 'A long time ago, back in the galactic wars. Me and my sister helped Ebanon relocate some of his people to Earth. We helped them get out and off their planet before there was too much loss of life. We essentially provided cover for their fleet so that they could leave. If it had not been for us, Ebanon would not be here now.'

'You have a sister Orion?' Said Isadora excitedly. 'You've never mentioned her before!'

'She died,' whispered Orion as he landed the small disk on Isadora's lawn. 'She didn't make it. One minute she was in the air and we were dancing round the big ships and causing a diversion. And the next I saw her falling from the sky and her craft exploding on the surface of Ebanon's planet. She was an excellent pilot. Even better than me. I still don't know how this happened.' Orion's voice had started to shake. He clearly found it very difficult to talk about this.

'I'm so sorry,' said Isadora touching Orion's arm. 'What was your sister's name?'

Orion swallowed. It had been a long time since he had spoken his sister's name aloud. 'Alana. Her name was Alana.' He said staring at Isadora with emotion in his face.

Suddenly he reached forward and touched Isadora's face. 'Sometimes you remind me a lot of her. I think you would have really liked her.' Tears formed in the corners of his eyes.

'If she was anything like you Orion, then I most definitely would have liked her.'

She leaned forward and gave the great Cowboy a hug.

'I cannot believe Ebanon did not help you when you asked him for help? After all you sacrificed for him?'

'Yeah I've thought about that often,' said Orion wiping these tears from his face and pulling back out of their embrace. 'Ebanon owes me big time. And the fact that he didn't help me when I asked him for help shows me one of two things. He is either really selfish and doesn't fully comprehend loyalty. Or he is really, really scared of Valdazar. In which case I guess I did him another favour as Valdazar got blown to smithereens.'

Isadora frowned. No matter how scared Ebanon was of Valdazar, he should have helped Orion. Orion lost his sister helping him out. She couldn't understand some people at all. Some people had such good hearts and would always help anyone in trouble. Yet for some people, it was just too much trouble.

She gave Orion another hug. 'I would always help you if you were in trouble Orion,' she said. Wiping fresh tears from the beautiful Cowboys face. He didn't make her as nervous anymore. He was like an old friend. She loved him.

'I know you would Miss Isadora,' said Orion smiling through the tears. 'You're my favourite Surface Human,' he sniffed.

They both laughed.

Final Plans

The next morning Peets met up with David and Aurora at the back of the exercise yard to finalise the plans of the breakout.

Peets had confirmed that he had spoken with Sylas the king of the Cockroaches and they were set for a breakout that night. The Cockroaches and the Bears would be waiting outside for Aurora to open the door to the facility around 12 midnight. The Cockroaches would then come in and take care of the guards and the Bears would help the general population of incarcerated humans get out of the facility and up to the Lava tubes.

'What about the portal Peets?' Asked Aurora. 'Do the Mantis know we are coming tonight?'

'Sylas said he would be talking to the Mantis last night to let them know that we will be coming to use the portal tonight,' said Peets nervously.

'And do we know where the portal is aligned tonight?' Asked Aurora.

'Ooh that's the best bit laughed Peets into Auroras head. The portal is aligned to Quential tonight! Somebody wanted you to get home!'

'Really?' Exclaimed Aurora! 'Oh my goodness thank the creator. This is the best news. I can't wait to see Mother and Father. Thankyou Peets so much for helping us. Are you going to come through the portal with us Peets? Then you can stay on Quential until the portal there is aligned to Delavia and then go back home then?'

'Yes,' said Peets, both excited and disappointed at the same time. 'I will come through the portal with you and then stay on Quential until I can get back home to Delavia. Mother and Father will have to wait a bit longer for my return,' he smiled. But both David and Aurora could tell by his demeanor that he felt sad and disappointed.'

'Don't worry Peets,' reassured Aurora. 'I will make sure as soon as we get to Quential that we find out when we can get you back to

Delavia. Mother and Father will be so pleased to see me. They will do anything for you!' Aurora laughed.

David had been quiet thus far. But now he began to speak. 'I wonder where Mother and Father will want to go? It's been 35 years since they left Earth. I wonder if they will still have family alive there? I wonder if they will want to go back to Earth? And if they do – what will we do? Where will we live? They've been gone so long, everything will have changed now.' The little boy felt scared. This place was all he had ever known. And now they were so close to escaping, he was suddenly afraid of the unknown.

'Do not worry my friend,' said Peets. 'You and your family will always be welcome to live in Delavia. There is plenty of room and Delavia is paradise.'

'And you will always be welcome to live in Quential,' assured Aurora. 'Quential is the happiest place ever. And I can teach you to fly!'

The little boy smiled at his two new friends. For the first time in a long time he felt a feeling of happiness. It was an unfamiliar feeling, but he liked it. He had made two new wonderful friends. His parents were alive. And they were breaking free. Life was good.

Home

Isadora slept for 6 hours straight when she got home. She did not remember any of her dreams and felt disappointed that she had not seen Adama again. It was lunchtime the following day when she started to stir. She was woken up by the sound of Mrs Stone crying in the next room over. Isadora sat up in bed and listened to the sound? Disorientated she rubbed her eyes. Yes that was the sound of her Momma crying. Isadora quickly got up and ran across to her Mommas bedroom.

'Momma what is it? What's wrong?' she asked concerned as she ran into her Momma's bedroom.

'I just miss your Daddy so much Isadora.' Sobbed Mrs Stone. 'I just miss him so much. I try so hard to get on as normal but sometimes my heart just breaks all over again. Where did he go? Why did he leave? He wouldn't just leave us Isadora I know he wouldn't. One minute we were all baking and the next he goes out to buy groceries and he doesn't come back? And they find his car and he's not in it? None of it makes sense!' Screamed Mrs Stone in grief. 'Where *is* he? I don't believe he's gone Isadora I just don't. And I don't believe he would ever leave us. So what happened to him? I feel so guilty because I feel so angry with him for leaving us. Why did he leave us on our own? I'm so lonely. I miss him so much!'

Mrs Stone sobbed and clung onto her daughter. She cried for the loss of her husband. She cried for the loss of her best friend. She cried for a daughter who no longer had a Daddy.

Isadora held onto her Momma and silent tears ran down her face. She missed her Daddy so much. Her Momma had been doing great since Orion had healed her. This was the first time she had seen her cry since Orion had helped. She hoped her Momma was going to stay healed and not get sad again and start drinking. She felt so guilty.

Her head had been in the clouds thinking about Adama all the time over the last 4 weeks and she hadn't really been there for her Momma.

'Do you fancy doing something together today?' Isadora asked. 'Just me and you. Something where we can remember Daddy together?' Isadora's voice broke and she began to cry too.

Mrs Stone pulled her daughter close to her and held onto her tight. 'I love you Isadora, I want you to promise wherever you are. You will always look after yourself. I couldn't Bear it if I lost you too. You are my world.'

'Don't worry,' said Isadora stroking her Momma's hair. 'I will make sure I am always safe.' she reassured. And if I'm not she thought, I have a direct line to the President of the United States in my pocket. She should laugh. But she didn't feel like laughing today. What had happened to her Daddy? Was he still alive? Would she ever find out? Fresh tears prickled her eyes and she let them fall.

Disappointment

So where did they go now thought Chinga. He had not given any thought as to what they would do if Peets was not there as he couldn't allow himself to think of that outcome. And now here they were. And Peets was not here. His Son was not there. Where was Peets? And Alana's daughter had been taken too? Why weren't they doing more to find her? It was all so strange. And what did they do now? Where did they go now? Peets could be anywhere. Chinga felt his chest tighten as he struggled to breathe.

What could he do? He had no idea where Peets was now. But he did know that Valdazar and the majority of the Valdons were still alive. And he knew that his daughter Sneets had seen Valdazar's telepath here today on this planet. Which meant that Valdazar was here. Why was he here? He must be after my family thought Chinga, because of what I have done. I don't know where Peets is so I cannot protect him. But I can protect the rest of my family Chinga resolved. I have to get my family somewhere safe instead of dragging them around the Universe and into potential danger looking for Peets. He had brought his family with him here to find his Son and Sneets had almost been captured by Valdazar again. Chinga could not lose another child. He just couldn't. He had to get his mate and daughter out of here and to somewhere safe. Somewhere where they would be protected. Then he would go off and journey and travel until he found Peets. And he would find Peets. But where was safe? Orion and Kaia would know what to do. Maybe he could leave Lamay and Sneets in Agartha until he had found Peets and then they could all go back to Delavia together. He must get word to Orion, Kaia and Isadora that Valdazar was still alive and most probably looking for revenge.

He was sure one of the scouting party had a Smart Glass pad. He wondered if it would work on another planet and he would be able to contact Orion. If he could contact Orion, Orion would be able to tell them when the portal here on Quential was aligned to Earth and maybe he could get his family safe in Agartha. Either way, he needed to speak to Orion and let him know about Valdazar. No matter what.

'Lamay, we need to go and re-join the scouting party and see if there is a way that I can contact my friends on Earth,' said Chinga sadly. 'They will know what to do.'

Chinga turned to the beautiful Alana and thanked her for her help.

'I will keep an ear out for your daughter on my travels, the Sasquatch assured. 'If I hear anything about her whereabouts, I will let you know.'

'Thankyou Chinga,' said the beautiful Elder with the Saffron hair. 'And if your little Son arrives here on Quential I will do the same.' They bade each other goodbye with sadness in their eyes and hearts.

As the family of Sasquatch stepped out of the palace of light and back onto the top of the mountain, Chinga scanned the horizon for the scouting party that had come with them. They had waited outside of the palace to give the Sasquatch family some space. Space that was not needed. Chinga felt anger rise in his chest.

'He is not here,' he shouted to the scouting party, sadly. 'Does anyone have a Smart Glass pad? I need to contact Orion.

And then we need to make camp for the night whilst we decide what we're going to do next.'

Breakout

David laid on his small cot in the dark trying to breathe slower. He had so much adrenaline coursing through his chest, he thought his heart might burst. It had been lights out since 10.00pm. And for the past hour and a half he had been running scenarios through his mind of how they were going to escape. He was so looking forward to seeing his parents again. Part of him almost didn't believe they were still alive until he saw them with his own eyes.

He thought about the Cockroaches and the Bears. Would they all be sneaking up on the facility now? Are they already in position? He trusted Koro with his life. But he did not trust Sylas the Cockroach King at all. He would throw his own people under the bus, let alone anyone else. What if he double crossed them? What if the Cockroaches didn't turn up? Would they still be able to breakout? What would happen if it all went wrong? *Calm Down* said a voice in his mind. You can do this. David started to breathe slowly and deeply and his little chest started to calm down gradually.

Suddenly a shape appeared at the bars of his cell. Quiet as a mouse. But he could feel her presence. Aurora.

'David are you ready?' Aurora said into his head. 'It is time.'

'Yes,' said David back. Getting up off his little cot silently. 'Let's go free my parents.'

Aurora focused on the lock of David's cell with her mind and slowly released it. Then David watched in awe as he saw the murky black shape of the cell door slowly open.

He was free.

He stepped tentatively forward into the darkness and reached for Aurora's hand. As he stepped into the hall of the cell area, a beam of light cascaded down upon them from the ceiling and highlighted their forms.

A girl and a little boy, off to save them all.

Earth

Human couldn't believe it. They had finally arrived at the Moon. This trip had seemed to take forever. Even though it had only taken them 4 days to get here. He could not believe that he was on the Moon and looking down at the Earth. This morning he was in the beauty of Quential and now he was in the stark space above the Moon looking down Earth. His home. He was so close. He knew how to fly the ship. All he had to do was get his wife and daughter and then lose the Valdons and escape.

'Can we go through the portal from here at any time to Earth?' Asked Human. 'Because there's no food on the Moon? And we need to get something to eat. Why don't we go down to Earth tonight and then we can find some cows and camp and then we're already on Earth in the morning for our mission? Master will be really pleased if we made up some time?' Convinced Human.

Greb and Than looked at each other and nodded. They were really hungry as they hadn't eaten at all whilst they had been on Quential. They had not managed to find any cows and were feeling really grumpy. They loved the Cows on Earth. They were super tasty. 'Yeah OK, we'll go down now and get some Cows,' said Than excitedly. And he began punching in the codes to take their ship through the portal system.

Suddenly a warning noise came up on the ship's computer and Human squinted to see what was going on. The ship's computer showed a picture of the Earth but with what seemed to be a huge orange barrier all around it.

'What does that mean?' Asked Human hurriedly.

'Means there's a barrier up. We can't get in.' Said Than. 'Masters not going to be happy.'

'A barrier up? How can someone put a barrier up around Earth?' Asked Human in sheer panic.

'Some planets have advanced technology,' Greb explained. 'They protect themselves from being invaded by putting up a technology barrier. It means we can't get in and no-one can get out. Without the barrier coming down.'

No, No, NO! thought Human. This can't be happening. His heart raced. How did he get to his family now? What could he do? The only thing I can do right now, Human sighed all hope leaving him. I have to tell the Master.

Human contacted Valdazar on the ship's computer. His Masters face came up on the screen. He looked happy. Valdazar thought they were going to tell him that they had the girl and the woman. They didn't.

'Sire, we have made it to Earth,' Human began.

'Yes, have you found the blond haired girl and the tall blonde woman?'

'We can't get into Earth to look for them Sire as someone has put a barrier up.'

'A what!' Screamed Valdazar. 'What barrier? Have you tried to get through it?'

'No Sire, the ship we are on will not even allow us to program in the co-ordinates. As it detects the barrier is there and shuts down our line of programming.'

For once Valdazar did not lose his temper. He sat stroking his black beard on his huge Serantium Throne. A thought came to him. A memory. He had an acquaintance called Ebanon. A tall Grey alien from one of the planets in Zeta Reticuli. He was sure that Ebanon had a base on Earth. Maybe Ebanon could help him? Of course Ebanon would help him he thought. He was Valdazar.

'Stay where you are Human and await further direction,' ordered Valdazar and his face disappeared from the screen.

Human's heart was racing. What did this mean? Well in the interim it means that my wife and daughter are safe as he can't get into Earth. So that is a good thing. Human started to calm down a bit. However it also means that I can't get back home to my family either. What is this barrier and who put it up there?

'So this barrier,' said Human to the Valdons. 'Does that mean no-one can get into Earth at all and no-one can get out either?'

Than rubbed his chin as he considered this. 'If there's a barrier up around a planet we can't go in with the ships. But if we were on another planet on foot, and the portals were aligned we could hop onto the Earth through a portal. But we'd have to do it individually through the portal one at a time. We can't take a ship in there as the barrier stops us from entering their air space.'

Human was quite shocked. That was almost an intelligent answer from the stupid Valdon. 'So if we were on foot, on another planet, and that planet was aligned to Earth, we could 'hop' to Earth that way through a portal? But we can't take the ship through as the barrier prevents it?'

Than scratched his head and thought for a moment. 'Yeah, we did that once when the master wanted us to take a planet that had a barrier up. Forgot what it's called. We had to go in one at a time until there was enough of us on the planet and then we took em' down that way. Then we located the technology and turned it off and Master brought in the big ship,' confirmed the green giant.

Human sat deep in thought. Maybe all wasn't lost. Maybe he could still get into Earth without the ship. But how would they escape without a ship. This wasn't *supposed* to happen thought Human in sheer panic. What did he do now?

'Wha we avin to eat then?' slurred Greb his tummy rumbling.

A Favour

Ebanon's Smart Glass pad winked and he picked it up and it molded to his hand. Slowly Valdazar's face emerged on the screen.

'Ebanon my old friend!' said the deranged man with the Black beard.

'Valdazar,' exclaimed Ebanon surprised. 'I have not heard from you in some time. We do not have any new technology down here at the moment. We are working on something new but it is not available yet.' Ebanon was trying to get rid of Valdazar as quickly as possible.

'It is not technology that I am after today, my skinny grey friend.' Advised Valdazar. 'I have a favour to ask. You may have heard of my recent 'situation' on Delavia?'

'I am aware that you took the planet yes.' Said Ebanon carefully. He did not want to anger this man.

'Yes, I did, I took it! It was mine! And then after I left a party from Earth came and blew up my old ship that I'd left there. And killed 20 of my Valdon soldiers.'

'I'm sorry to hear that Valdazar,' said Ebanon wondering where this was leading. I did not aid them he thought. Valdazar can have no grudge with me here.

'Yes, it was all very frustrating. However nobody messes with me. I am Valdazar. And I want that planet back. And I will take it back again. It will not be difficult. The people there are pushovers. However I must deal with this Isadora Stone and Kaia woman who have shown me so much disrespect. They must be dealt with.'

Ebanon could now see where this was going. 'You intend to punish Isadora and Kaia for the part they played in taking Delavia back?'

'Yes Ebanon' smiled Valdazar, his teeth all yellow and stained. Bits of meat stuck out of those teeth from every angle. Trapped and festering. 'And I need you to help me.'

'What is it you need me to do?' Sighed Ebanon.

'I need you to get me the Isadora Girl and the Kaia Woman. That is all. Just bring them to my empath who is stationed just above Earth and he will bring them to me. My Empath also tells me that there is a barrier around Earth at the moment. Why is this?' Valdazar sneered.

'I don't know why the barrier was put up Valdazar,' informed Ebanon. 'But I do know who controls the barrier. I will contact them and ask that they remove it briefly so I can get the two humans to you.'

'Excellent, excellent' said Valdazar. 'And how do you intend to capture these humans for me?'

'I know where they will be,' sighed the tall grey alien. 'These Humans are known to me. I will speak with my Raptor friends and see if they will create a diversion for me.'

'And will you be doing this tonight Ebanon?' Said Valdazar with menace in his voice.

'Of course Valdazar, as you wish. I will contact you when I have them.'

'I look forward to hearing from you' smiled Valdazar and his face disappeared from the screen.

Valdazar sat smiling to himself.

Now to make Human aware of the plan.

The Plan

The ship's computer winked on Humans small craft. Valdazar's face came into view.

'Never fear Human, your trip has not been in vain,' smiled his Master. 'I have contacted an old friend of mine. Ebanon of one of the Grey's factions. He is aware of who Isadora Stone and Kaia are. He is going to capture them and bring them to you on the ship. Once you have them. Let me know and I will bring my ship to meet you. It will only take me a matter of minutes to get there in the new ship as you know,' bragged Valdazar.

'So stay there and await Ebanon, and he will bring you the humans. Then contact me and I will come. Did you get all that Human?' Said Valdazar patronizingly.

'Yes Sire,' confirmed Human. We are to wait here until Ebanon brings the Humans and then I am to contact you. And you will come here Sire.'

'Yes Human, Yes! I must say, I have trained you well! You are proving to be a most loyal and helpful servant.'

'Thankyou Sire' said Human in an emotionless voice.

'Keep me updated,' snapped Valdazar and his face winked from the screen.'

Human's heart and mind raced. They were bringing his daughter and Kaia. But what about his wife? He couldn't escape without his wife. No, NO! This was not happening. What was he going to do now?

'So what we goin to eat then?' Grumbled Than. 'How longs this goin to take, I'm starving!'

Breakout

Aurora and David walked very slowly and silently down the hallway that separated the two rows of cells. At the end, fast asleep sat the guard. David felt his heart beat faster in his chest in anticipation of what could happen. Closer and closer they inched to the guard. David felt sure that the sound of his heart beating so loud, would wake up the guard. But as they slowly passed by him, like two silent ghosts, the guard slept on.

Aurora pointed out the huge front door to the facility as they passed by it on foot. That was where they would let the Cockroaches and Bears in once they had freed David's parents.

As they passed by the huge front door which looked like a gigantic, silver garage door, the sandy steps to the lower levels of the facility became visible. The upper levels were all silver and metal as they had been built upon the surface of the planet. The lower levels had been dug out of the inside of the planet and in view of this, it was like stepping down into caves. Little spot lights had been placed in the cave ceiling above the stairs and suddenly Aurora and David could see a lot more clearly. David had never been down these stairs before. He had always done his work on the upper levels of the facility. Aurora was brought down these stairs daily to converse with David's parents so she knew where she was going.

Aurora spoke into David's head. 'We must walk slowly and carefully down these stairs. The room where the guards are in is diagonally to the right of the bottom of these stairs one we get to the bottom and turn down the corridor. She reiterated. So when we get to the bottom of these stairs we turn to the left and face another corridor. To the right on this corridor is the room with the guards where I will put up the false image that we can walk behind. At the end of this corridor, also on the right, are your parents.'

David nodded his head and took a deep breath. Aurora and David begin to walk slowly down the flight of sandy stairs. David counted the steps in his head as they descended downwards. 1,2,3. Anything to keep his mind off of the anxiety that he felt in his chest. As they climbed down lower and lower, the temperature got cooler and the guard's voices got louder. David had counted to 30 by the time they reached the bottom of the stairs. Aurora put her figure up to her lips to remind David to be really quiet now. David nodded his head. He thought he might be sick.

Aurora let go of the little boys hand and walked slowly down the new corridor and up to the edge of the new room. David could not see what she was doing. To him it looked like she was just stood there in silence. Suddenly she stepped fully into the space opposite the doorway of the room that the guards were in and outstretched her hands.

'Come on!' she shouted into David's head. 'I can't hold this image for long! It drains my energy!'

David jerked into motion and began to walk towards Aurora, slowly and steadily. He was almost up to where she was. He started to panic. Surely the guards would see him? Cold sweat trickled down his back and he started to shake. But thoughts of his parents entered his mind and he carried on walking. Even though every fiber of his being wanted to run back up those stairs and get back into his safe and familiar cot. He was now opposite Aurora and as he stepped into the space in front of the doorway, he could see a table full of guards laughing, drinking, smoking and playing cards. Fear ran up his spine. Could they see him? David froze.

'Keep going!' Shouted Aurora into his head, 'I can't hold this for much longer David!'

The sound of his friend's anguish broke through David's fear and he moved past the doorway and into the corridor beyond.

As soon as David did this Aurora quickly dropped back across to the other side of the doorway and let out a huge steady breath.

Suddenly David heard one of the guards say. 'What was that? Did you hear something in the corridor?'

No, No! Please don't come out here David thought his mind racing with fear.

'Shut up Coggings!' shouted another guard. 'Stop trying to make excuses because you are losing! Get on with it! Your hand!'

'I'm not!' Shouted Coggings indignantly. 'I thought I heard something in the corridor.'

'Of course you did,' said the second guard sarcastically, 'now play.'

David and Aurora held their breath hoping that the guards would resume playing their game. What if they came out into the corridor and saw them? They were so close to breaking free! David's chest heaved up and down and he prayed to God to help them in this moment.

'It was obviously nothing,' said Coggings bashfully and placed his hand down on the table.

The guards all laughed and started jeering when they saw the hand that Coggings had. It was a bad one.

'Sounds in the corridor ey Coggings!' They laughed 'yeah right! Ha Ha!'

Aurora had gathered enough of her strength back now and gestured for David to move down the corridor. Down and down they went. The corridor got darker towards the end. And more damp and fusty. Finally they got to the end pen.

Were his parents in here thought David excitedly? He squinted in the dim light to catch a glimpse of them. He could see two shapes laid on the floor close together. Yes! They were there!

Aurora began working the door open with her mind. First the lock. Then the gate swung open and back into the corridor.

David flung himself into the room and ran over to his parents.

As he dived on his Mother and Father in jubilation, his Mother let out a muffled scream. The last time someone had come for her in the night they had taken them away from their little boy.

'Shhhhhhhh,' said David, 'Mother it's me! It's David,' he whispered. 'I've come to free you but we must be quiet. We must not alert the guards.' David put his finger up to his lips.

David's Mother and Father looked at their Son in the dim light in astonishment. How had this happened? How had David found them? Thank god. Their Son was here. They were together again.

David, and his parents sat and hugged each other and cried silently. So much relief. So much Love. The little boy hugged his parents so tightly. He would never let them go again.

Suddenly David heard Aurora's voice in his head. He had almost forgotten that she was there.

'David, we have to go.'

The Raptors

Once again whilst Isadora was sleeping, there was a blinding flash of white light and she was back again in Agartha. She had taken in recent times to going to bed fully clothed as she never knew what might happen. Also since Adama had told her that he was keeping an eye on her whilst she was sleeping, she didn't fancy wearing her old nighty to bed. One minute she was asleep and the next she was sat in the huge Council meeting cavern again. This was the cavern where she had originally been portalled into in her first Council meeting and had met Parmeethius.

She found herself once again sat opposite the curious looking purple humanoid. Parmeethius began to speak.

'Miss Stone, you have met with your President and informed him of our situation down here, and thankfully, it appears that digging has stopped. For that, we Delo are grateful. Thank you for that Miss Stone.'

Phew thought Isadora, it worked! Thank you Mr President!

'However,' Parmeethius continued. 'The digging from the surface has unsettled the Raptors and still they will not retreat to their original hunting grounds. It has unsettled them so much that we are still at risk here. Something must be done. Also I have recently been informed that some sort of barrier has gone up around the outer airspace of the Earth. So we are no longer able to get to the Galactic Market to exchange our goods. This is unacceptable and the President must be informed and it must be taken down.' Parmeethius turned to Kaia. 'Kaia, what do you suggest we do in order to obtain control here in Inner Earth? Now the Raptors have been disturbed it has altered our way of life down here. My people are scared that they cannot walk around our own homes for fear of a Raptor invasion!'

'Parmeethius,' Kaia began in her calm, sweet tone. 'The Raptors cannot penetrate our boundaries, our technology is too strong. It has kept them out for millions of years! Yes I know it is unsettling to think that they are just outside our borders, but they cannot enter. You know this my friend.'

Parmeethius frowned. 'Yes I know this well Kaia, but this digging from the surface has created a problem. It is not too bad here because of where you are situated. But where The Delo lands are, there has been much digging. The Raptors are forever pacing back and forth outside our territory, waiting for one of our kind to come out. It is unsettling for my people Kaia! And also for yours! This cannot be tolerated! My people.....'

Suddenly a huge high pitched scream echoed around Inner Earth from the great hall outside.

'Ahhhhhhhhhhhhhhh, help, help us! The Raptors have breached the Portal!'

Everyone at the Council table leapt up as one in shock.

'How can this be?' Shouted Parmeethius. 'Kaia – I tried to warn you – but you would not listen! Now terror will rain down upon us! Seal the door quick!' he shouted. Babu, the green lizard man, who Isadora had never heard speak once, ran across the room and sealed the door with what looked to be white light. The white light came out of the lizard man's hands.

'Parmeethius No! My people need help! We need to help my people!' Kaia screamed.

'If we go out there now, we will all be dead Kaia. We can help better in here,' he shouted. 'Is the Crystal here?'

Kaia stared at the purple elephant man, 'Yes Parmeethius, the Crystal is here!'

'Fetch it quick! Let me contact my people. My Delo Army. Time is of the essence. If we get them here quick, there may not be too many casualties for your people. Fetch the Crystal now!' He screamed.

Kaia disappeared under the table and then brought out a huge pale pink Crystal. She lifted it with ease as if it was light as a feather. But to Isadora it looked like it was very heavy indeed.

Kaia placed the Crystal on the table in front of Parmeethius.

Parmeethius looked into the great Crystal. The great pink Crystal lit up as if it was on fire.

'Larken, we have been breached here in Agartha by the Raptors. You must bring our army. Bring all our Technology. They have just come through. There is time to save many. Leave some warriors behind to protect our borders, but bring as many as you can spare. Do not waste time.' Parmeethius said as more screams were heard outside the Council room. 'Hurry!'

Isadora heard another voice say. 'Yes Parmeethius, we are on our way.'

Parmeethius looked at Kaia. 'Where will all your people be at this time of night?'

Kaia put her hands on the table and looked like she was about to cry. 'The children will be either having a short rest, or with the animals. We do not need to sleep for very long here in Agartha as you know. But they may well be resting in the caves or in the technology rooms, or tending the animals. There is no need to seal any of our rooms Parmeethius. There is no need to seal our rooms here.' Kaia looked aghast. 'The Elders will be walking in the fields or in the technology rooms. Or in the great hall just outside here. There are not many of us and we go where we please.'

'Hopefully not too many of the Raptors will have broken through,' Parmethius paced as he considered what to do next. 'I think...'

Laser Fire was heard in the area outside the Council Hall and shouting. Isadora heard a huge guttural shriek. One which she had never heard before in all of her 15 years.

'What was that?' She shouted.

'Raptors Isadora,' Orion said upholstering one of his weapons. 'And a mighty big one I should wager. That is the sound of one that's just been hit. Kaia, do any of your people have weapons on them at the moment?'

'Only our people who manage our borders,' Kaia said trying hard not to cry. 'But there won't be many of them inside of here tonight. They will be outside maintaining our perimeter. And we don't send many out there as we know we can't be breached. Our technology is sound and has been for millions of years. I do not understand what has happened here!'

'But if the portal has been breached?' Orion began and his voice trailed off. No-one wanted to consider what would happen if the portal had been breached.

Suddenly the huge pink Crystal lit up again and a familiar voice began talking. Isadora recognized this voice.

'Orion my old friend, Are you there?'

Orion raced round to look at the Crystal.

'Ebanon? Ahhh now's not the best time for a conversation my friend!'

'Yes, Yes I am aware of that. I understand that you may be needing some help right now?'

Orion laughed nervously, 'Ahhhh yes, we've just been breached by Raptors! We're not too sure how many have got in yet, or HOW they have got in. We're waiting for re-enforcements from our friends here the Delo.'

'Yes, of course, I'm sure the Delo will help you with your *situation*. However might I suggest that it is prudent that we get Miss Stone out of there? And Kaia as well?'

'I think it is very kind of you Ebanon to offer your help to Miss Stone and I'm sure that Orion would agree', interjected Kaia. 'However I will not be leaving my people. My place is here with my people.' She said whilst rubbing her hands over her forehead. 'As soon as our friends the Delo arrive I will be going to help my people,' the beautiful priestess explained.

'Of course,' said the gangly grey alien. 'Orion I can bring my ship to Agartha now and pick both you and Miss Stone up? Providing Kaia gives me the necessary clearance of course?'

'Yes of course Ebanon,' said Kaia. 'I would fly her out myself but right now we are not near our ships and Parmeethius has sealed the door.' She said looking pointedly at Parmeethius.

'No need Kaia,' smiled Ebanon with his tiny mouth. 'I will happily help your friends. Consider this repayment of the debt I owe you Orion.'

'Errr yes. Yes Ebanon, sure,' said the huge Cowboy.

'Shall I meet you in the centre of Agartha where the ships come in and out Orion, the great hall I think you call it? How far are you from there?' asked Ebanon.

'The room we are in is just off from there Ebanon so yeah we can meet you there. Are you coming now? How long will it take?' The huge Cowboy looked worried.

'A matter of minutes Orion providing I have clearance to enter Agartha. I will come through the cavern wall. I will set off now,' the grey alien finished. The beautiful pink Crystal once again winked off.

'Kaia,' Orion said. 'As soon as I've got Miss Stone here to safety I will come back and help out here.'

'Thank you my friend,' said Kaia and touched the great Cowboys arm. 'Thank you for your help Orion.'

'No problem Ma'am,' smiled the beautiful Cowboy. He turned to Isadora. Now Miss Stone. 'How do you feel about shooting you some Raptors?' He winked.

Ebanon

Babu had unsealed the door of the Council Meeting room and Orion and Isadora stepped slowly outside. Orion had given Isadora a gun! Well a gun of sorts. He said it fired lasers! Isadora had never fired a gun before in her entire life. She knew many people at her school that did. Some people even went shooting animals for sport back home. But her Momma and Daddy had never owned a gun. Her Daddy used to love animals and would never hurt one. And Isadora would never want to shoot another living creature either. Not unless she had to. Maybe she could if her life depended on it.

'Stay behind me now Ma'am,' whispered Orion. 'We'll take it nice and slow. Maybe there was only one and they already got it.' He drawled inching further and further down the long cave wall that opened out into the main way fair of Agartha City.

As they slowly stepped out into the bright light of the great hall in Agartha City, Isadora's heart dropped. She quickly counted. She could see five large Raptors spread out among the beauty of the main City. Two she could see walking slowly through the crops and grassland. One was trying to scale a beautiful statue that the Agarthans had as their main focal point of the area. It was a statue of a Mother and a Father and a child all hugged together and looking out over the land. To Isadora it represented family and unity and it was beautiful. This Raptor was currently trying to eat it, seemingly not realising that the figures were not real. Another Raptor was kicking around what looked to be some sort of fruit. It was as big as a Watermelon, but the skin was blue in colour. That's no watermelon, Isadora thought in her shocked mind. The final Raptor was more of a problem. It was stood directly in front of them with its back to them, almost as if it was waiting for someone.

'Don't make any sudden moves now Ma'am,' Orion whispered. 'When Ebanon's ship arrives, hopefully it will knock that one over,' Orion drawled, 'and then in the element of surprise we can quickly run into the ship and get the hell out of here.'

'OK' Isadora whispered. She was frozen with fear. The only time she had ever seen anything like this was on Jurassic Park. And that movie had scared her half to death. And now she was here with five Raptors and the only thing that stood between her and them was Orion.

Isadora and Orion stood holding their breath, waiting for Ebanon to arrive.

Suddenly laser fire streaked into the cavern.

'What the?' Orion said as he braced himself against the tunnel wall, then looked back out into the cavern. 'Ah shoot!' he drawled as the Raptors turned towards the laser fire.

Isadora watched as five Agarthan Warriors ran into the cavern and started firing at the Raptors. The Raptors screeched and started running towards the warriors. The lasers seemed to wound them, but not mortally as the Raptors were still running straight for the five warriors. The Raptors had such scaly skin, the lasers didn't seem to be able to penetrate too hard. It scorched their skin, but not much more.

'Ah shoot, old Orion's gonna have to get involved now. My weapons *will* kill these creatures,' he said smiling at his gun. 'Well of all the worst timing! You stay here Ma'am said Orion tipping his cap. These fellas need my help!' And he ran off behind the retreating Raptors and began firing.

Isadora watched in horror. Orion's weapon, whatever it was, seemed to work on the Raptors. He had already taken one down. The one that had been nearest to them. As Isadora's eyes focused on Orion, her heart stopped. One of the Agarthan Warriors that had entered the great hall was Adama.

'Oh god please no!' she screamed wracked with fear. Instinct took over and she moved out into the great hall and after Orion.

She watched as the four Raptors ran to the four Agarthan Warriors and her Adama. Orion was running after the Raptors and had taken another one down. That left three. The Agarthan Warriors' weapons were just pinging off the three remaining Raptors. Suddenly the three remaining Raptors split ranks. One ran up to Orion and Orion blasted him. The Raptor fell. But two of the remaining Raptors were bearing down on the five Agarthans. There was no time. She would not let anyone hurt Adama. Isadora looked at the weapon in her hand and made a choice. She lifted it up and aimed at one of the Raptors that was currently bearing down on Adama. What would happen if she hit Adama! No, no this could not be happening. Suddenly Orion fired and took down the Raptor that was the nearest to Adama. The Raptor fell. That just left one. Isadora started running towards the Raptor that was left and screamed 'NOOOOOOO'. The Raptor looked up at Isadora and started running towards her, its jaws open. It jumped through the air towards Isadora.

Both Orion and Adama shouted 'NOOOOOO' at the same time. As the Raptor jumped through the air at Isadora. Orion leapt through the air and shot the Raptor in the belly. It lurched once towards Isadora, and again, and then fell to the ground. It was done.

'Isadora!' Adama shouted and ran up to her. He fell on the ground dragging her with him and hugging her.

'You were trying to save me?' He said with tears in his eyes. 'Thankyou. You distracted it. Thankyou. I thought it was going to eat me!' He grabbed hold of her face and kissed her tenderly on the mouth. 'How will I ever repay you?' He smiled, pushing his long dark curly hair behind his ears.

'Ah – this works' she laughed. And he kissed her again.

Suddenly a huge grey disk burst through the cavern wall and hovered above the ground. A door opened on the disk and several small grey steps cascaded out of the ship and down to the floor.

The tall grey alien reached a hand out of the ship, 'Quickly my friends get in, there may be more Raptors inside yet!' Ebanon shouted.

Orion chucked his weapon to the Agarthan Warriors. 'Isadora, give me your gun my darlin, they will need these if there's any more of these things in here.'

Isadora gave Orion his gun and he passed it to the Agarthans. 'The Delo are on their way my friends, they will help you contain the situation from here. Adama, I've got this now. I'll make sure Isadora gets home safely,' Orion reassured.

'If it's OK with you Orion, I'd like to make sure that Isadora gets home safely too,' Adama said, looking deep into Isadora's eyes. 'I will come with you.'

'Quickly,' shouted Ebanon, 'in case any more Raptors make it through! Let's get Miss Stone out of here!' The Grey Alien reached out his clammy hand.

'OK,' said Orion looking perturbed. 'Let's do this!'

And Isadora, Adama and Orion leapt up the small grey steps and into Ebanon's ship.

Breakout

Aurora, David and his parents walked slowly and quietly back down the corridor and towards the guards room once more. As they got close to the doorway, Aurora gestured for them to stop. She then used her mind to create the false image of the corridor wall again. With her hands held in front of her she called once more to David.

'David pass quickly, I can't hold this for long!'

David grabbed hold of his Mothers hand and began to pull her across behind Aurora. His Mother froze with fear and shook her head. Terror etched into every feature of her face.

'It's OK,' mouthed David,' trust me!'

David's Mother allowed herself to be led past the open door of the guard's room and to the other side. David's Father followed slowly behind. They had no idea what this girl was doing. But somehow the guards were not able to see them. Then as soon as Aurora felt they had passed, she jumped to the side and let out a slow and silent breath.

This time Aurora did not wait to gather her strength, she pressed on. Beckoning them all, she began to move quickly and silently back up the 30 sandy steps that would lead them back out to the surface level above. There was no time to lose now. The most difficult part of the mission had been accomplished. They were almost there!

As they reached the top of the steps. Aurora quickly checked that the guard was still asleep. He was. Aurora gestured for her companions to stand in front of the huge silver door whilst she began concentrating on the release button.

'Hey what are you doing?' Shouted a familiar male voice. 'Stop them! They're trying to break out! Wake up!'

David recognized the voice instantly. Nathan! His cell was one of the nearest to the guard at the front. He must have been awake. No!

Quickly Aurora jumped to action and unlocked the main front door with her mind. The huge silver door jerked slowly into action making a loud metallic squeal.

The guard who had been slowly starting to wake up, quickly galvanized himself as to his horror he saw the main door starting to open. He grabbed his radio and punched in an alert to his boss Eldon. Then he leapt forward and hit the emergency button which halted the opening of the main door.

A slow evil smile spread across the guard's face.

'Thought you could escape? There is no escape from here. You'll be...'

Everybody flinched and ducked as the main door was ripped off its hinges by several huge, great, furry, paws.

David and his family turned around to face the cold night air.

Standing outside, as far as the eyes could see were Bears and Cockroaches. There were hundreds of Bears. And Millions of Cockroaches. And right at the front, smiling in the light of the stars was his friend Peets.

'What are you waiting for!' He shouted, 'let's go!'

Realisation

Isadora, Orion and Adama sat down in Ebanon's spaceship and began to fasten themselves in. The huge grey disk headed towards the cave wall of Agartha.

Don't worry Isadora thought closing her eyes, you know they don't crash, they can somehow go through the wall. But she had begun to shake with the release of adrenaline. Her teeth felt like they would chatter out of her head.

'Ebanon, we need to get Miss Stone home as a priority please, Orion began. 'We need to get her back home to her Momma. It's been a hell of a day!' He smiled. His smile fell as he noticed Isadora and Adama were sat next to each other on the ship holding hands.

'Of Course my friend of course,' said Ebanon. 'But I hope you won't mind. I need to stop off at Dulce first and pick something up that I think Miss Stone might find useful in future?'

'What's that Ebanon? Orion drawled. 'I think the only thing that Miss Stone would find helpful right now, is a wink of sleep!'

'Yes, yes,' Ebanon laughed. 'I'm sure you are all very tired. And I know you want to get Miss Stone back quickly and get back to your friends in Agartha Orion. But as you informed me, your friends the Delo are coming. They are sending reinforcements! All is in hand Orion. I have something that I would personally like to give to Miss Stone. A short stop off at my base will not hurt I'm sure. It will only take a few minutes Orion?' Said the tall gangly alien jovially.

'I'd like to get back to my people as soon as possible.' Interjected Adama. 'I need to make sure that they are all OK?'

'Of course my friend,' assured Ebanon. 'A quick stop off at my base. Then we will get Miss Stone home and then I will take you back to Agartha.'

Suddenly the ship winked into a large bright, white room.

'We are here my friends,' smiled Ebanon.

The door opened and the small silver steps filed out.

'Follow me!' The huge grey alien said.

Trapped

Ebanon led the three friends into a small white room. It had two small white sofas and a table. On the table there seemed to be a selection of human food. Biscuits, sandwiches and some glasses of water.

'Now if you will please allow me a moment whilst I go and fetch my gift for Isadora,' the grey alien smiled. 'Please help yourself to some food!'

Ebanon left the room and closed the white door behind him.

Orion looked at the table 'He calls this food?' He drawled lifting up one of the sandwiches and sniffing it.

Isadora smiled and looked at Adama. 'Adama what happened? We were in the Council room, we only heard screams? And Parmeethius said it was a Raptor breach. Was anyone hurt?'

Adama frowned. 'There were only two of the Elders in the great hall when the Raptors came through. They saw them come through and managed to run and make it to the rest of us who were over in the Technology room. We then sealed that off. According to them, the Raptors walked through the main portal. There were only the five that came through, and then the portal sealed itself again'

Orion turned round to face Adama with a mouthful of sandwich, 'Through the main portal?' He spat as he swallowed his sandwich down. 'How could they come through the main portal? They don't have the technology to do that? He drawled. The Raptors don't have technology?'

'I know said Adama, so someone let them in.' Adama stood up and walked towards Orion. 'Before we five came out to take the Raptors, one of our scouts from the perimeter made it through to us. They said they heard the screams and that's why they came running in.

But no Raptors had passed them Orion. And they were out on the far perimeter of our lands. Way beyond the portal entry.'

Orion swallowed. 'So someone got those five Raptors in there through the portal and bypassed your scouts?' He sat down on one of the white sofas and stretched his long legs out. 'Who would do that?'

'I don't know,' said Adama. 'But someone let them in there.'

Suddenly Orion's chaps began to flash. He reached inside and took out his Smart Glass pad. It molded to his hand. Within seconds Chinga's huge orange face filled the screen.

'Chinga!' Shouted everyone. 'Good to see you. Have you found Peets?'

The gentle Sasquatch's face crumbled. 'No,' he cried silently. 'He is not here. He is not here.'

'I'm so sorry my friend,' said Orion sadly. 'We really hoped he had gone there. We could try the place the portal should have gone before and after Quential next!' Said Orion trying to give the sad Sasquatch some hope.

'Yes, that is probably a good idea,' said Chinga numbly. 'But I need to get the rest of my family safe first. That is why I'm calling. My daughter Sneets has seen Valdazar's telepath here on Quential and a Valdon ship. My mate Lamay tells me that Valdazar and his army were not on that ship that General Myers blew up Orion! Valdazar left the day before we got there on another new ship that he had acquired through a trade. So when General Myers blew up that huge black spikey ship, he basically just did Valdazar a favour by getting rid of his old empty ship. Nothing was on it.'

Orion, Isadora and Adama looked at each other in disbelief.

'So Valdazar is still alive?' Said Orion in shock.

'Yes,' confirmed Chinga, 'and my Sneets has seen his telepath here today on Quential and if his telepath is here then *he* is here. He's probably looking for us in revenge for the part we played in overthrowing the remaining Valdons. I need to get my family to safety Orion and off this planet. I can't be worrying about losing Lamay and Sneets too. It's hard enough being parted from Peets. If I know that Lamay and Sneets are safe, then I can concentrate on looking for Peets. Can you give me a safe place to locate my family on Earth whilst I find Peets?' Pleaded the Sasquatch. 'It looks like I'm going to be looking for my Son for a little while longer.'

'Sure my friend,' said Orion, 'but ah, we're in a bit of a situation ourselves at the moment. Agartha was just attacked by the Raptors and I'm just in the process of getting Miss Isadora here home. Once I've got her home. I will contact you my friend and we will sort out getting you and your family back here safe. Just hang tight where you are and I will be back in touch as soon as I can OK?'

'Thanks Orion,' said Chinga, 'you are a real friend.'

'No problem buddy,' said Orion and Chinga's face winked off of the Smart Glass pad.

'I can't believe Chinga hasn't found Peets said Isadora rubbing her face anxiously. It's been 4 weeks now.'

'I know,' said Orion. 'I hope to god that little guy is alright.'

Ebanon

Ebanon looked at his Smart Glass pad and contacted Valdazar. An image of Valdazar ripping into a leg of some sort of huge bird, filled Ebanon's screen.

'Yes!' Spat Valdazar spraying the screen with chunks of meat. He wiped his arm hurriedly over his mouth smearing meat into his black beard. 'Do you have them? The girl and the Kaia woman?'

'I have the girl,' spoke Ebanon slowly. 'Kaia...would not come.'

'What?' Valdazar screamed. 'What do you mean she wouldn't come? Do you ask her *nicely*?' Valdazar leered. 'I didn't expect you to *ask* her Ebanon?' The crazy man shouted. 'I asked you to *take* her! By any means necessary! I thought we had an understanding here Ebanon!'

'Valdazar, you must understand,' began the grey alien. 'Our faction of Reticulans have lived on Earth for many years now and since the humans came, we have co-existed relatively peacefully with the ones on the surface. The original humans of Inner Earth have tolerated our presence here on Earth as we have not put their existence in jeopardy. Yes there have been skirmishes shall we say from time to time. But for the most part. There has been peace. We do our thing and they do theirs. I also have an *understanding* in place with Orion from Alpha Centauri. And these two humans are friends of his. So I am risking a lot here Valdazar to help you out. When/If Orion works out that I am the one who let the Raptors through the portal, I will be breaking an *understanding* that I had in place with him. So please understand I have done the best that I can for you without making it obvious that I have betrayed Orion. Orion is not to be messed with. He is very connected. Both on this planet and off. He knows many powerful people, on many planets.'

'As powerful as me!' Screamed Valdazar! 'I am not to be trifled with,' the deranged man howled. 'I will rage vengeance down on ALL who stand in the way of what I WANT!'

'Yes, my friend, yes,' assured the tall grey alien. 'And I have most of what you want. I have the girl, and I also have another Agarthan who jumped on my ship with her. Once I get these two to you, I am sure you will be able to barter the boy for Kaia. Kaia has a good heart. She will gladly swop places with the boy so the boy can live.'

'Who is this *boy*?' Sneered Ebanon. 'Why did he get on your ship with her?'

'I do not know his name. I have not seen him before. But him and the girl seem to be.....close.'

'Close?' Laughed Ebanon. 'What does that mean?'

'They look like they have some sort of affection between them,' the grey alien considered. 'You know how humans do, before they procreate.'

'Procreate?' Said Valdazar quizzically. 'What does procreate mean Ebanon? Stop speaking in riddles!'

'Mate, Valdazar. The affection they have for each other before they choose a mate!'

Valdazar considered this for some time. Slowly he began to smile, a slow, evil, smile. 'You mean they *like* each other he sneered?'

'Yes,' Ebanon sighed the grey alien in exasperation. 'I believe they *like* each other.'

'Well, well, well,' smiled Valdazar rubbing his hands together. 'Now doesn't that make this all the more interesting?' He laughed. A slow, murderous laugh. 'My telepath tells me that there is a 'barrier' of some sort up around Earth, and he cannot enter with his ship. Otherwise I would have sent him down to you to collect the humans. You will need to bring the humans up to him. What is this barrier and can it be removed?'

'Yes, yes I am aware of the barrier of course,' Ebanon said nodding his head.

'I am aware of who has put the barrier in place. I will make contact with them and ensure that it is lifted momentarily so that I may bring the two humans to your empaths ship as you request.'

'Good, good,' said Valdazar. 'Yes, yes I am in fact quite pleased about this turn of events. As soon as you have delivered the humans to my empath, let me know. I may decide to make a surprise visit to Earth myself and give them a welcome party.' And with that Valdazar disappeared from the screen.

Ebanon stood and rubbed his chin. He walked up to the huge white Crystal that was in his private room. It was time to make contact with the true powers who ran planet Earth. It was time to contact 'the voice.'

Breakout

Aurora quickly leapt forward and pressed the emergency release button of the cell doors. Everyone's cells pinged open. 'What's happening?' shouted someone.

'We're breaking out!' Shouted Aurora. 'Everyone follow us! The Cockroaches and Bears are here to help us!'

The guard who was still in shock suddenly sprang into action and reached for his gun.

There was a high pitched squeal from the nearest Cockroach who dove into the facility and picked up the guard by his head and started shaking him around in his mouth.

'David, come on!' Shouted Peets.

'Yes, Mother, Father, follow me,' shouted the little boy and he ran towards Peets.

Aurora checked to make sure that the people were starting to come out of their cells and shouted 'Follow us to the Lava tubes. We are going to portal off this planet! Quickly follow me!' Then she ran to catch up her friends.

As a slow stream of people started to follow David and Aurora out of the Facility. The Cockroaches all began to pile into the place. The guards from downstairs who had heard the commotion were greeted by thousands of angry Cockroaches. Their screams filled the night.

'Quickly!' shouted Aurora back at the line of people who were leaving the facility. 'We are making our way to the Lava tubes and we are going to portal off this planet to another one where we will be safe. The Bears will help us. Follow the line and we will lead you to the tubes!'

Peets and Koro at a steady jog led the line of people all slowly spilling out onto the red sand of Mars. Followed by David and his family and Aurora. Hundreds of Bears dotted the landscape and helped guide the scared people from the facility and into the line that would guide them to the tubes. On and on they jogged.

'How far are the Lava tubes?' shouted David as his little chest threatened to burst.

'They are not too far,' shouted Koro the kind Bear. 'You see that hill over there?' Said the large Bear pointing at a pointy structure not too far in the distance.

'Yes, I see it,' shouted David.

'That was once a volcano,' shouted the Bear as he galloped along. 'The Lava tubes are in there. We climb down through the top and then into the tubes. The Mantis will then show us where the portal is.'

They carried on jogging towards the hill that housed the entrance to the Lava tubes. Back at the facility the screams of the Cockroaches could still be heard. David shuddered. They jogged and jogged putting more and more distance between them and the screams of the guards.

Without warning the sound of laser fire peppered the night. Huge streaks of bright green light shot through the air and glanced off the hard red floor.

Everyone looked up at the night sky in horror. A huge dark ship hovered in the sky. Eldon. The guard had managed to make contact.

'Quick run, everyone run!' Shouted Koro. 'We must make it to the Lava tubes!'

Everyone began running at speed now. Panic coursed through the air. Screams filled the night. The smell of burning and fear and terror.

David ran as fast as his lungs would allow him with his parents close by. Not too much further now.

Peets and Koro led the line. They were almost at the entrance to the hill. All of a sudden a huge green laser beam streaked through the sky and hit Koro in the side. The large Bear groaned and fell.

'NOOOOOO!' Shouted Peets. 'Koro, Get up! Get up! We're almost there! Koro *please*, get up! We're almost there!'

The huge Bear smiled at Peets as the light started to leave his eyes. 'Keep running little one. You are almost there. You must finish this journey for both of us.'

'NO!' screamed Peets. No! Please No, Koro get up you can make it! We can heal you when we get to Quential. Please!'

'Peets he's gone!' screamed David, 'we can't help him now. The entrance is there! Quickly we have to go now! Otherwise Koro will have died in vein! We need to escape!'

David's Father upon realising that David would not leave without this orange furry creature, picked up Peets and began running with him to the Lava tubes.

'No,' screamed Peets, he's not dead! Please don't leave him. Koro get up!'

The last thing that Koro saw as he closed his eyes for his final sleep was his little orange friend being carried down into the Lava tubes by David's Father and screaming his name.

'You did well little one, whispered the Bear. Almost home now. Almost home.'

Betrayal

Orion was pacing up and down in the small white room like a caged animal. The frustrated alien was muttering under his breath.

Adama and Isadora exchanged worried glances.

Suddenly Orion stopped with his hands on his hips and let out a huge deep breath. 'That Son of a ....hoo hoo, Miss Isadora now I am pissed. Now I am mighty angry!' He turned to face them.

'What?' Said Adama, trying to work out where Orion was going. 'What are you thinking?'

Orion took off his Cowboy hat and threw it into the tray of sandwiches.

'Ebanon' he said slowly in a low deep voice. Isadora had never seen Orion like this before. He was furious.

'Ebanon?' Said Isadora. 'I don't understand. Ebanon what?'

Orion stalked off to retrieve his hat and plonked it back on his head.

'Ebanon let them in,' said Orion slowly and full of fury. 'Who else? Don't you think it's funny that he just happened to contact us and offer help when we had only just been breached by the Raptors? Why would he do that? Ebanon never does anything for anyone unless there's something in it for him. So what's in it for him? I'm so sorry Miss Isadora, I've let you down. I so badly wanted to get you out of there and to safety. I think I played right into his hands.' Orion reached into his holsters for his weapons and came up dry. 'Ah sheeeeeet!' He screamed and the Cowboy hat got slung again. 'I goddam gave my guns to your people Adama. We have no weapons here?'

'I still have my laser,' said Adama as he patted his right thigh.

'With all due respect Mister Adama, they didn't help you out too good the last time you used them did they?'

Adama coloured up. 'That's just because the Raptors have harder skin than we anticipated. We've had no need to war with them before Orion. Our kind have never fought the Raptors before today. We've always lived in peace and respected each other's boundaries!'

Orion stalked up to the door and tried to open it. He tried with his hands and then it looked to Isadora as if he was trying to open it with his mind. The huge Cowboy stared at the door. Nothing budged.

'What do we do Orion?' Said Isadora panicked. 'What would Ebanon want with us here?'

'If you remember Miss Isadora, Ebanon asked for you and Kaia!' Orion fumbled with his chaps and brought out his Smart Glass pad. 'He wants the pair of you. And my guess is this is something to do with his *friend* Valdazar! And I'll be damned if I'm letting any harm come to either of you.'

Orion stared intently at the Smart Glass pad shimmering on his hand. 'Come on, Come on Sir, and please still be awake!'

Adama and Isadora hovered over Orion's shoulder. An image of the ceiling of the White House came into view.

Orion cursed again. 'He's gone to bed. Of all the nights we need him to be awake and he's gone to bed.' Orion rubbed his mouth trying to think of who to contact next.

'The President!' Said Isadora quizzically.

'Yes Miss Isadora. Your President could help us out of this hole we have found ourselves in here. He has a Joint Special Command Team who know where this base is in Dulce. They could be here within minutes. IF WE COULD REACH HIM!' Orion shouted.

Suddenly Isadora remembered. She frantically started searching in her pants pocket. 'Please be here, please be here!' Suddenly her hands connected with what she was looking for and she pulled it out excitedly.

'The phone!' She exclaimed. 'The phone the President gave me for emergencies. I can call him!'

'Yes Isadora yes,' laughed Orion. 'Yes call him quickly we haven't much time.'

Isadora hit the button on the phone and waited as the phone rang once, twice, three times.

Time stood still.

On the fourth ring, the muffled voice of the President of the United States answered the phone.

'Miss Stone do you know what time it is? I was having an early night – for once!'

'Sir I'm so sorry, I would not have used this phone if it wasn't an emergency. Sir we need your help...'

Back Down

Chinga, Lamay and Sneets had been sat waiting for Orion to contact them back for what seemed like an age. Where was he? What was he doing? This was all taking too long! Chinga needed to get his family back to safety before they were taken *again* by Valdazar. Plus they were really thirsty as due to the surprise appearance of Valdazar's telepath this morning, Sneets had been unable to collect water. Everyone was now extremely thirsty as they had not drunk all day. They *needed* to get some water. Chinga also thought that it would be wise to be near the portal on the mountain when Orion made contact as that would be how they got off this planet. But that was near where Sneets had seen the Valdon ship. Chinga listened to the sound of his tummy rumbling and felt how dry his mouth was.

'Come on,' he gestured to Lamay, Sneets and the scouting party. 'We need to get water otherwise we will all become too weak to move and then we will be no good to anyone. There's a great chance that Valdazar is further down this mountain so we need to keep our wits about us in order that we are not captured. But we must get water. So I suggest we start walking back down the mountain now to find water as near as we can. Keep your eyes and ears open and be as quiet as possible. We do not want to alert anyone of our presence in advance.'

Everyone slowly began to get up and pack up their things.

Chinga was tired, thirsty and hungry and he was missing Peets more than ever. But he had to get his family to safety. And he had to find some water for everyone as they were all parched.

The party set back off down the mountain with anticipation in their tummies.

The Lava Tubes

David's Father carried Peets down into the Lava tubes and set him on the ledge inside. David's Mother and David quickly followed behind. Peets had stopped struggling now. It was too late. He just felt numb. The best friend that he had ever had was just been gunned down before him and there was nothing that he could do to help. If it hadn't have been for Peets' stupidity in coming to this planet, his friend Koro would still be alive. He would never forgive himself.

'Where's Aurora?' Said David in panic. He had not noticed her for a while.

'I'm here!' she shouted climbing over the ledge of the hill and down into the tubes.

'What do we do now?' asked David's Mother in a panic.

'I don't know!' Said Peets wiping his nose on his arm. Koro was the one who knew where the portal was. And now he's dead.'

'Let's keep walking down the tubes!' shouted Aurora. 'We're bound to bump into a Mantis eventually and they will show us where we need to go!'

'OK,' shouted David and they all set off walking downwards into the long dark tube. As their eyes became more accustomed to the darkness, they began to see better. In the distance further down the tube they could see a shape. A tall gangly shape. A Mantis.

The huge Mantis was reddish brown in colour and stood the full height of the tube itself. It held a very large golden stick with a swirling white ball on the top.

As they walked closer to the Mantis, Aurora connected with the being telepathically.

'My friend, we have come here today to use your portal. In agreement with the Cockroaches and Bears we have broken out of the human facility and passed control over to them. We have been assured safe passage and use of your portal off the planet.'

The Mantis did not speak. It did not move.

Aurora tried again. 'Sylas the Cockroach King has assured us that we may use your portal tonight to leave this planet. Time is of the essence. Eldon has come back and is shooting at everyone who is leaving. Please! We need to leave now!'

The Mantis spoke telepathically into Auroras head. 'There is **no** agreement in place with Sylas the Cockroach King. He has no say over who uses our portal.'

Aurora spoke to David and Peets telepathically. 'He says there is no agreement with Sylas for us to use their portal!'

'I knew it!' Shouted Peets in exasperation. 'I knew we should never have trusted that disgusting Cockroach!'

'What's happening!' said David's Mother in fear. To them it just looked like everyone was stood in silence.

'OK,' said Aurora trying to calm herself down. 'Let me barter with him. I may be able to do something.' She looked back at the Mantis and connected telepathically. My name is Aurora of Quential. I am a high priestess on my planet and Guardian of the Crystal. If you help us get back to Quential today, my parents who are the Elders on the planet will be indebted to the Mantis of Mars. They will give you anything you want.'

The Mantis looked thoroughly unimpressed.

Suddenly Peets had an idea. He spoke telepathically into the Mantis' head. 'My name is Peets. I come from a place called Delavia. It is famed throughout the Cosmos for its honey. Our bees are some of the oldest in the Universe and they make honey from Delavian flowers which are the most beautiful flowers in the Universe and they produce the sweetest nectar. Our honey is also excellent at curing ailments. Any ailments you have can be cured by this honey. If you let us pass through your portal today. You have my word that as much Delavian honey as you can eat – is yours.'

The Mantis considered this offer. He had heard of Delavian honey. It was quite the delicacy in the Universe.

'Peets of Delavia, said the Mantis telepathically. As much honey as we can all eat?'

'Yes!' said Peets excitedly. 'You can have Delavian honey for life! An alliance between our species! And you can come and collect it when you want as you have access to the portal!'

The Mantis bowed his head to the furry little Sasquatch.

'A deal has been reached. An alliance has been made. We will come to collect our honey within the next few days. You may pass.'

The huge gangly Mantis moved to the side to reveal a shimmering bubble of light.

'Yes!' Said Peets happily. 'OK everyone all you have to do is walk into the bubble and you will come out of the other end at Quential. Follow me!'

And with that Peets jumped into the bubble and disappeared.

David looked at his Father and Mother and they all jumped through together.

Aurora turned around and shouted to the rows of people who were making their way down the Lava tubes.

'All you have to do is jump into the shimmering bubble and it will take you to my home planet and away from here. Pass this message on to everyone who is behind you! Follow me!'

And with that Aurora jumped into the shimmering bubble and disappeared.

The Delo

The Delo Army had arrived in Agartha and had secured the area. There were no more live Raptors within Agartha. It was established that the portal was working correctly and had not malfunctioned. The area was now secure. So that left the question. How did the five Raptors get in? Fortunately there had been no casualties. No loss of life at all. It was almost as if the Raptors had come in just to create a diversion of some kind. But for what?

Larken the head of the Delo army was currently discussing the situation with Parmeethius and Kaia.

'Why didn't they move further into the City if their purpose was to take over this territory?' Asked Parmeethius. He could not understand it.

'Maybe they could not see well in this light,' suggested Kaia. 'We know that Raptors do not do well in sunlight as their eyes have adapted to hunt in the dark?'

'Yes that is a possibility,' agreed Larken. 'However it does seem strange that they just stayed in this one area near the portal and in the main square. As this is the brightest area. You would think that if their intent was to take over Agartha territory that they would have moved further into Agartha where it was darker and they could operate better.'

'Yet they stayed in this area in the main square in front of the Portal?' considered Parmeethius staring at one of the huge Raptors that was currently lying dead on the ground. 'It doesn't make sense. Why hang around here in front of the portal? And how did they get in through the portal? We've established that it is working correctly? So how did they get in?'

Kaia considered this. 'Someone must have let them in. Someone who knows how a technological portal works. That would have to be someone who is familiar with Technological portals. For instance someone who also has a Technological portal themselves.'

Kaia and Parmeethius stared at each other and both said at the same time 'Ebanon.'

'Why would Ebanon let the Raptors in?' asked Parmeethius quizzically.

'When he contacted us on the Crystal, he asked for Isadora and for me to join him on his ship. Do you remember?' She reminded them.

'Yes,' said Parmeethius. 'But what would the head of The Greys want with you?'

'I don't know, but we need to warn Orion and Isadora fast,' said Kaia starting to walk to the Technology room.

'Adama got on the ship too,' shouted one of the Agarthan soldiers.

Of course he did, thought Kaia as she started to sprint to the Technology room. Isadora is on that ship!

Quential

Peets, David, Aurora, David's parents and the incarcerated humans who had made it out of the facility all began to pop out of the portal on the side of the mountain on Quential. One by one they popped out of the sky. The portal was about 10 feet in the air so there was a drop upon landing. Peets was not expecting that. But luckily there was a huge patch of moss underneath the portal that was very soft and bouncy and due to this, no-one seemed to be to be injured at all.

Peets jumped up and shook himself off. He scanned around him for David and Aurora. Both were on the floor smiling and rubbing their bottoms.

'I've never had to portal into my planet before' smiled Aurora. 'I had no idea the portal was in the sky!' She spoke aloud for the benefit of everyone.

'Yes!' laughed David's Mother. 'You might have mentioned that Aurora!'

'Sorry!' Aurora laughed! 'Now quickly everyone. I will lead you up to the top of the mountain and to my home. There is water on the way if you are thirsty. But we need to move fast. I want to get us all up to the top of the mountain before nightfall!'

The elation that Peets felt upon escaping from Mars did not last long. He suddenly remembered his friend Koro and fresh sadness bloomed in his chest. What could he have done to stop that from happening? No-one knew that Eldon was going to return when he did. That wasn't his fault. But he could not stop thinking about the fact that Koro would never have been killed, if he hadn't have been helping Peets in the first place. Everywhere he went, everything he did. He kept messing up. He tried so hard to be a good person and help people. But he kept getting things wrong. He had made a huge mess of everything. And now here he was on *another* strange planet.

Still separated from his family. And his friend Koro had died helping him. Fresh sorrow ripped through his heart. Why did Koro have to die? Tears dripped down his fur and soaked his chest.

Aurora walked over to the little Sasquatch and hugged him.

'Your friend Koro loved you. And he was brave. If it hadn't have been for Koro, none of us would have got out of that place. Koro is a hero. I will make sure that he is remembered as such on Quential for all eternity. The Bear who brought back the Princess.'

Peets smiled a sad smile. 'I miss him already' he said in a quiet voice.

'I know,' Aurora smiled sadly. 'But Koro would be so happy to know that you made it to safety. That's all he wanted.'

She gave the little Sasquatch a huge hug.

'Now come on, we need to get you home. My parents will be able to find out when the portal is aligned to Delavia. They have a portal map in the palace.'

'OK,' said Peets quietly.

And the party of bedraggled people began the long walk up the mountain of Quential.

Aurora led the march with love in her heart. She was home!

Help

Orion, Isadora and Adama sat and waited in the white room. The President had assured them that help was on the way. And to sit tight. There was not much else that they could do at this point. They sat in silence in anticipation of what would happen next.

There was a commotion outside. The three friends looked at each other in earnest as they could hear shouts and the sound of breaking glass. Laser fire rang out through the air.

Isadora felt herself start to shake again. Adrenaline coursed through her body. Was this the President's men who had just arrived? Adama grabbed hold of her and held her close to him with one arm. In the other he held his own weapon poised and ready and locked on the door.

They stood and waited to be found. Intense laser fire ricocheted around The Greys base and shouting and screams. Were the Presidents men winning or were The Greys winning?

'Goddam it, let me out and give me a weapon, I can help!' shouted Orion at the door.

Suddenly there was the sound of a pop. And the door handle started to smoke. Next the door opened and in came a man dressed head to foot in black and carrying a weapon of some kind. He had a helmet on and Isadora could not see his face. As he spoke his voice sounded like it was magnified in some way.

'Follow me please,' said the man dressed in black and he led them out into the large room outside. Isadora had to step over many, many Greys. Orion and Adama protected Isadora from any stray laser fire as they followed quickly behind the man in black who was leading them out of the facility. Isadora could see at the far end of the room Ebanon the huge tall grey alien was in a battle with another man in black. Light shot out of the palms of Ebanons hands at the man in black, as the man in black in turn shot back with his weapon. Ebanon's head flicked up and in their direction as he saw his captives escaping. Fury etched in his face. Valdazar would be livid.

Isadora concentrated on following Orion and the man in black with Adama protecting her from behind.

Finally they passed through the room and into the room they had originally come into when they first visited Ebanon's base.

The man in black shouted, 'Jump through the wall.'

As they had all done this before they knew what to expect. Orion jumped through first and then Isadora and finally Adama. They were back in the dark corridor that led off from the high speed underground rail track.

'Follow me!' shouted the man in black and they all trailed out of the dark corridor and into the brightly lit underground railway area.

A medium sized silver disk floated in the air above the railway tracks with silver steps leading up into it.

'This way!' shouted the man in black and began running up the steps and into the ship.

Orion. Isadora and Adama followed the man in black up into the ship.

The first thing that Isadora heard as she climbed up into the ship was the voice of the President.

'Well Miss Stone,' said the President, 'it's about time we got you home!'

Valdazar

Valdazar paced up and down in front of his throne. This was taking too long. Ebanon should have contacted him by now. Perhaps there was an issue with the barrier?

'Human,' the crazy dictator shouted, 'bring me my Smart Glass pad! I need to find out what is *taking* so long. I am not accustomed to *waiting*. This is unacceptable!' Suddenly Valdazar realised that Human wasn't there. He had done this many times over the past 5 days it had taken Human to get to Earth. He had quite missed Human. We should have just taken my new ship Valdazar mused. We would have gotten there in no time. But I have to look important he considered so I must send people to do things for me.

A gigantic Valdon ambled in holding his Master's Smart Glass pad on the palm of his hand. In the gigantic Valdon's hand it looked the size of a postage stamp. Valdazar snatched it from his hand and began to contact Ebanon. Valdazar stared at the pad on his hand. The picture swirled and swirled and then the inside of a white room became visible. There was no Ebanon. It was deserted.

'Arrrrrgh!!!' Screamed Valdazar in a guttural, feral scream. 'Something is wrong. Ebanon is not there. And he would not leave his Smart Glass pad behind.' Valdazar sat on his throne and slowly ran his fingers through his beard.

'I must deal with this situation myself,' Valdazar whispered under his breath. The time has long since passed that I must return to Earth.'

'I AM VALDAZAR!' The psychopath screamed. 'And *no-one* will make me look a fool. YOU!' Valdazar screamed and pointed at the nearest Valdon.

The Valdon jumped, 'Yes Sire?'

'Ready the entire Valdon Army and all of our ships. We are going to Earth. Barrier or no barrier. Nothing will stop me from taking that planet.'

Reunited

Chinga and his family trudged back down the mountain with sadness in their hearts. As they passed the houses of their new fairy, gnome, pixie and elf friends, all came out to see the Sasquatch family and congratulate them on their reunion. One look at the sadness in the faces of their large, furry friends told them that the reunion had not happened. Peets was not at the top of the mountain. All the beings of the Quential Mountain felt sadness for the Sasquatch family. Rows and rows of little pixies, elves and gnomes took off their hats as a sign of respect to their new orange friends. All of the little fairies floating in the air turned out their lights in a show of solidarity for the loss of their new friends. They felt the sadness along with them too. For they were all one.

Suddenly there was whispering and muffled shouts. A wave of excitement ran round the little people. They had seen something that Chinga had not.

Another party of people were walking up the mountain. These people looked very disheveled indeed. They were wearing tatty clothes and they looked tired and weary. There was a mass of grey looking bodies moving up the mountain. With a little streak of orange at the front.

Cries of 'He's here!' rippled up the mountain through the little people. Passed like a chain of Chinese whispers.

Sneets saw him first. 'Look Father,' she said in anticipation. 'That looks like a Sasquatch?'

'Yes Love,' said Chinga. 'Let's just get back to the water. We need to get some before we all fall down,' he said sadly.

'Father!' Screamed Sneets at her robotic parent. 'It's a Sasquatch the same size as Peets! Peets!' Sneets shouted, knowing in her heart that it was him. 'Peets its Sneets!' She began running down the mountain towards her brother'

Peets looked up at the sound of his sister's voice. Could it be?

Then he saw her. He saw his sister running as fast as her chubby little legs could carry her down the mountain and towards him.

The two little Sasquatch began running through the trees to each other. Could it really be them? As soon as Peets and Sneets saw each other they jumped into each other's arms. Lamay started crying and running towards her children. 'Peets! Peets oh my boy we found you!' She gathered both her children up in her arms and swore that she would never let them go again. Never again.

Chinga stared at his Son like he had seen a ghost. Could it really be him? It was like this wasn't really happening. He could see his children and his wife hugging but he couldn't move. He was frozen with fear.

'Father, Father!' Shouted Peets in astonishment. 'I made it back to you! I knew I would find you, I knew I would!'

Peets flung his hairy little arms around his Fathers legs. He could not believe that his family were here. God was smiling down on him. In all of the places that his family could be in the Universe. They were on the one planet that he had escaped to.

Chinga looked down at his Son. 'Peets, Peets my boy, is that really you?'

'Yes Father, Yes! It's me! Look!' The little Sasquatch said as he pulled his Fathers fur.

Chinga fell to his knees on the floor and stared into the eyes of Peets. And suddenly the dam burst. Floods and floods of tears streamed out of Chinga's eyes. 'I thought I would never see you again my Son, I thought I would never *see* you again. And it's my fault because you watched me go through the portal to the honey planet. It was all my fault,' He sobbed.

Peets began to cry too. He had cried so many tears for Koro he thought he would never be able to cry again. But being reunited with his family was all too much. Fresh tears gushed out of his eyes.

'I'm so sorry Father,' cried the little Sasquatch. 'I should have done what Mother told me and stayed in the caves and waited for you to come back. But I thought I could help!'

Lamay and Sneets came and joined Chinga and Peets on the floor and they all hugged and cried and laughed.

In the excitement of the reuniting of the Sasquatch, no-one had noticed that the missing Princess had in fact returned as well.

Suddenly a gnome noticed Aurora. Cries of 'She's back! The Princess is back!' Filtered through to Peets' ears.

'Father,' said the little Sasquatch remembering his friend. 'Aurora is with us too! She was on Mars with us!'

Chinga pulled back and looked at his Son in astonishment. 'You've been on Mars! Oh my boy. Oh my brave boy. And the Princess is here too with you? Aria will be over-joyed. This is better than I ever could have wished for. Thankyou creator!' Chinga screamed at the sky in happiness.

The creatures of the Quential Mountain gathered around the Sasquatch family and their Princess and they cried too. Tears of joy. For they had their Aurora back home. The Princess had returned.

What a day this was. A day of legend. A day that would be celebrated throughout the ages.

Reunited once more.

The Fleet of Valdar

The entire Valdon fleet was making its way from Valdar to Earth. Valdazars new ship had incredible technology which allowed them to make the journey in no time at all. The rest of the fleet however was using an older technology and it would take them five days to traverse the portal network and make it to the next Galaxy over. The Milky Way in which Earth was situated. The same as it had for Human, Greb and Than.

On his own personal ship, Valdazar had 1,000 of his best Valdon warriors with him. The Valdons were incredibly tall and 1,000 was the most that Valdazar could transport across the Cosmos with him, without them being cramped. Even so, the presence of 1,000 Valdons in armor sat in close proximity at any one time made Valdazar feel incredibly edgy.

The 1,000 Valdons had all been loaded into the ship and were ready to go. Valdazar was just about to talk to Human again and realised once more that he was not there. No matter, thought Valdazar, he is waiting for me outside Earth and I will have him back with me again soon.

Valdazar punched in the location of Earth on his ships computer and the huge ship rose up into the air and hovered. Suddenly a shimmering wormhole appeared in front of Valdazar's ship and in a matter of seconds the enormous ship had disappeared. Finally it is time to go back to where I started thought Valdazar. But this time I am a mighty conqueror!

Home

Peets, Sneets, Chinga and Lamay. David and his parents, Aurora and all the incarcerated humans from Mars made their way up the mountain and to the palace of light. It was taking them so long as every creature that they met on the way wanted to welcome their Princess home and also congratulate Chinga and his family on being reunited once more.

In the end Aurora laughed and said, 'I will come and hug you all, each and every one I promise I will, but first I must let my parents know that I am home.'

Finally, the party of friends made it to the top of the mountain and the palace of light. Aurora raced off in front in search of her parents.

'Mother, Father!' She shouted as she raced into the palace. 'I'm home!'

Chinga and his family caught up just in time to see Aria walk in and see her daughter for the first time.

'My daughter!' Aria screamed and ran to Aurora.

'Mother!' cried Aurora and her strength left her. She fell to her knees.

Aria and Aurora hugged each other on the floor of the palace of light. The Sasquatch family and all the creatures of the Quential Mountain cried as they witnessed this special moment. Finally the Princess had been returned home.

'Where is Father?' asked Aurora finally pulling back from her Mother.

'Your Father has taken the ship and is out looking for you,' said Aria wiping tears from her daughter's face. 'We could not sit here and do nothing. I waited here in case you came back. And here you are!'

'We must let Father know that I am home!' Laughed Aurora. 'I will contact him through the Crystal!' She jumped up and ran over to the huge white Crystal that was in the middle of the palace of light.

As Aurora placed her hands on the Crystal, it began to light up and shimmer. 'I am pleased to see you too my friend,' said Aurora to the Crystal. 'Now I need to let my Father know urgently that I am home. Can you connect to the Crystal on his ship please?'

The Crystal shimmered and flickered and suddenly a man's handsome face appeared in the Crystal.

'Aurora!' he gasped. 'Are you home? Oh my child. Are you OK? Are you home safe? How did you get home? Did they bring you back or did you escape? Where have you been?'

'We escaped Father! My friend David and his friend Peets helped us all escape. There's lots of people who came with us Father who are from the planet Earth. They took me to Mars Father and there were lots of humans beings held there against their will. I've brought them all back with me. Can they stay here if they wish?' Aurora asked with hope in her voice.

'Of course they can!' laughed Aurora's Father. 'They can stay forever! Oh my girl you are home. Is your Mother OK?'

'Yes Mother is here Father and she is fine!' Laughed Aurora.

'Tell your Mother I am coming home my love. I am on my way.'

And the face of Aurora's Father blinked out and the Crystal returned to normal.

Aria walked up to Lamay and embraced her. 'And I see you have your Son back too! How has this happened? Aurora come and tell us everything!'

Aurora, Peets and David began to fill their parents in right from the very beginning of when Peets arrived on Mars and met Koro. Each filled in their part. Peets broke down when he described the Love and help that he had received from his friend Koro the Bear. If it had not been for Koro, Peets would probably not be here now.

'I wish we could have met Koro my love said Lamay in tears. We owe him so much. He gave his life in order to deliver you back to us. How could we ever thank him enough?'

'I know' said Peets. 'I will never ever forget him. He is the best friend that I have ever had.'

'And what now?' said Chinga. 'You said that Eldon's ship came back and it was that ship that shot Koro? Will Eldon come back here with his ships and try and take this planet again? Especially when he knows that Aurora is missing?'

Aria frowned. 'I think the time has come to ask for help. We are a peaceful planet. We do not know or understand the ways of war. But we need to be able to protect ourselves. Chinga, is there anyone that you know that can help us? We need to be able to protect ourselves if Eldon and his army come back. I will not lose my daughter again.'

Chinga nodded his head. 'Yes I'm sure my friend Orion will be able to help us. He seems to know a lot of people. He will know someone who can help protect your beautiful planet. I love this place!' Chinga smiled. 'And now my Son is back I feel like I can finally enjoy being here. There's no way I would let anyone hurt this planet. I'm expecting a call back from my friend Orion. As soon as he calls. I will ask him what can be done.'

'Thank you my friend said Aria from her heart. I feel very lucky that the creator has brought you to our wonderful planet.'

'And me too,' said Chinga with love in his heart. 'Our children are home! The creator has answered our prayers! And now we must ensure that we can defend our planets and keep our families safe. My friend Orion will know what to do.'

Back Home

Isadora sat in the JSOC spaceship with Orion, Adama, The President of the United States and three men in black.

'Gosh,' she thought. 'My life is so surreal.'

'So Isadora,' said the President. 'What was that all about?'

Isadora sighed and ran her hands through her hair nervously.

'We found out tonight from our friend Chinga who is currently on a planet called Quential, that Valdazar is still alive Sir. We thought that he had been killed when General Myers blew up the ship. But apparently he had already left a day prior in another ship that he had recently been traded. He took the majority of his army with him in that ship so Valdazar and the Valdons are still at large. We believe that Ebanon – the leader of The Greys was trying to help Valdazar by kidnapping me and Kaia. Only he didn't get me and Kaia. He got me, Orion and Adama,' smiled Isadora.

'Why would Valdazar want you and Kaia asked the President, I don't understand?'

'I don't know,' said Isadora wearily. 'Maybe he blames us somehow for losing his control over Delavia. I genuinely have no idea. But it was me and Kaia he wanted.'

'And why didn't Valdazar come and get you himself if he's such a great and powerful conqueror?' Asked the President quizzically trying to make sense of everything. Not that he wanted Valdazar turning up at his planet or anything. But none of this made sense?

'Again Sir, I don't know.' Said Isadora. 'Maybe it was just easier to get Ebanon to transport us to Valdazar.'

'What are your thoughts Orion?' said the President to the alien Cowboy.

'I don't know Sir. All I do know is when I've asked Ebanon for help in the past in taking Delavia back for Chinga. Ebanon would not help me as he said he had an 'understanding' in place with Valdazar. So I believe the two of them are friends.'

'And you young man said the President to Adama, I don't believe we have met before. Who are you?'

'I am Adama of the Agarthans,' said Adama. 'It is a pleasure to meet you Sir,' said Adama politely.

'Likewise!' said the President jovially. 'So what's your take on all this Adama?' asked the President.

'My gut tells me that Valdazar is behind everything Sir. And I believe he used Ebanon to let the Raptors into Agartha.'

'You've had Raptors in Agartha. Crikey you've been busy tonight!'

'Yes Sir,' said Adama wearily. 'It's been an eventful night.'

'We're here Sir,' said one of the men in black.

'Miss Stone we are back at your home,' said the President. 'Keep that phone on you and if anything happens at all where you feel unsafe, you call me OK?'

'Yes Sir', smiled Isadora. She was back home. It had been such a scary night but she did not want to leave. She did not want to leave as she was not sure when she would see Adama again. And Orion.

Adama leaned in to hug Isadora and kissed her on the cheek. 'I will see you again soon Isadora, I promise' he whispered.

Orion stood up and pulled Isadora into a bear hug. 'I will see you soon Isadora. You stay safe for the rest of the Summer you hear. If anything ever happens and you need me, you shout 'Orion' in your head telepathically. I *will* hear you.'

'OK, said Isadora tearfully. Don't leave it as long next time. You didn't contact me for 4 weeks last time. And...well I missed you guys!'

'We won't Isadora said Adama, I promise.' He winked at her.

'How about me Miss Stone,' said the President jovially. 'Do I get a hug too?'

'Errrr, 'said Isadora unsure of what to do next.

'I'm just joking Isadora,' said the President laughing. 'I'm sure hugging the President is most 'uncool'. Don't forget what I said about that phone,' the President said seriously. 'You need me, any time of the day or night, you call me OK?'

'Yes Sir,' Isadora smiled warmly at the President. 'I will.'

She took one last look at the occupants on the ship and Adama and then slowly stepped out of the ship and down the silver circular stairs.

Tears prickled her eyes, but she would wait until she got inside her house before she cried.

She missed Adama so much already. And Orion.

They both felt like home.

Valdazar

One minute Human was looking out over the peace and quiet of Earth. It looked like a giant, beautiful, green, blue and white pearl.

The next, his Master's huge ship appeared in space above Earth, narrowly missing taking their ship out.

And so it begins thought Human.

His Master's ship sent out a beam of light which was calling their ship in. Human's ship began to slowly return to its Mother ship. Valdazar had arrived today and in five days, once the Valdon Army had traversed the portal network. The entire Valdon Army would be here.

So I have five days thought Human, before I am dealing with the entire Valdon Army. Five days before there are a thousand of these huge stupid creatures ready to descend on Earth.

As Human's small craft was being drawn into the Huge Valdon war ship, he had mixed emotions.

He was elated that he was almost home. His heart soared at the prospect of seeing his daughter and wife again. However he was horrified that he was working for someone who was on a quest to hunt down his daughter. He had to find a way to overthrow his Master. But how? Human tried to quieten the fears in his mind that created slow steady trickles of sweat that pooled at his spine. I am in the best place to help my wife and daughter as I am with the enemy. And he has no idea *who* I am. Valdazar confides in me. He tells me practically everything as I am the only one around here who speaks any sense. I am involved in all of his plans. I had the opportunity to escape him once before because he trusted me. It was only because of that barrier that I am still here. His mind went to the barrier. The barrier itself was both a blessing and a curse. A blessing as it was keeping Valdazar away from his family. And a curse as it was also stopping his return to them. But Ebanon did say there was a way to take it down and he knew who had put it there in the first place? If the barrier is up then at least my wife and daughter will remain safe. If the barrier is removed then I have to find a way to rescue my family and escape Valdazar. I will find out the Masters plans. He trusts me and uses me in everything. I am well placed to learn his secrets, and then I can act. There is plenty of time to take him down. Keep alert and watch *everything*. Learn how to navigate the main ship. His master was that erratic, he was bound to make a mistake sooner or later, and Human would make sure that he was ready.

All I have to do is watch and wait.

Tears filled Humans eyes at the task that lay ahead.

I'm coming home Catherine. I'm coming home Isadora. Daddy is coming home baby girl. Just sit tight.

The End (For now!)

Thank you so much for reading my second book in the Isadora Stone series. Even as I finish this one I will be starting to write the third book in the series, so please do keep a look out for that!

The third Isadora Stone book will continue on where we left off with Valdazar now being stationed outside Earth's barrier. The third book's adventure will be focused around the beings in the oceans of the Earth. So Mermaids! Yippee!

A big thank you to everyone who reads my books.

It really does mean the world to me.

Much Love

Laura Anne Whitworth